FURY
and the
WHITE MARE

by ALBERT G. MILLER

Cover illustration by Lydia Rosier

SCHOLASTIC BOOK SERVICES
New York Toronto London Auckland Sydney Tokyo

Books by Albert G. Miller available
from Scholastic Book Services:

Fury, Stallion of Broken Wheel Ranch
Fury and the Mustangs
Fury and the White Mare

No part of this publication may be reproduced in whole
or in part, or stored in a retrieval system, or transmitted
in any form or by any means, electronic, mechanical,
photocopying, recording, or otherwise, without written
permission of the publisher. For information regarding
permission, write to Holt, Rinehart & Winston, CBS
Educational Publishing, a division of CBS, Inc., 521
Fifth Avenue, New York, NY 10017.

ISBN 0-590-31295-2

Copyright © 1962 by Albert G. Miller. All rights re-
served. This edition published by Scholastic Book Services, a division of Scholastic Inc., 730 Broadway, New
York, NY 10003, by arrangement with Holt, Rinehart
& Winston.

12 11 10 9 8 7 6 5 4 3 2 1   9   2 3 4 5 6/8

Printed in the U.S.A.   06

Contents

Chapter 1
THE WILD WHITE MARE

Pete Wilkie, the scrappy old foreman of Jim Newton's Broken Wheel Ranch, lay in bed fast asleep. The grin on his face indicated that he was having one of his "happy" dreams.

"Ever since I was knee-high to a snake's chin," he had once told Joey, "I've on'y had two kinds of dreams: happy or turrible. I cain't figger it out, Joey; I never have any of them in-between kinda dreams, like reg'lar folks do."

In Pete's "turrible" dreams, which were always the same, he found himself being thrown from a bucking bronc before the eyes of a jeering rodeo crowd. These dreams usually ended by his falling out of bed.

His "happy" dreams, on the other hand, were assorted. In some of them he was the world's champion trick rider and roper, in others he was owner of the

King Ranch in Texas. But in the happy dream that Pete was enjoying this cold February night, he had discovered a uranium mine and had money enough to buy everything that had ever caught his eye in the Western Section of the mail-order catalogue.

"Let's see now," he muttered in his sleep. "I think I'll buy me one of them Stetson hats with the five-inch brim. Mebbe I'll even order two of 'em, seein' as how they're only a measly ninety dollars apiece."

Joey Newton had somehow come into the dream, and was looking over Pete's shoulder. "Lookit here, Joey," said the old man, pointing to the catalogue. "It says here this hat's got seven x's on the sweat-band. That means it's the best doggone top piece money kin buy."

Joey whistled softly. "Boy, Pete, it must be great to be as rich as you are."

Pete chuckled. "It shore is. Say, Joey, is there anythin' special you got a cravin' fer? Jest name it an' I'll buy it fer you."

Joey thought for a minute. "Gosh, Pete, I can't think of a thing I want. But look, how about buying something for Fury?"

Pete snorted. "Now what in tarnation would you buy fer a horse that's already got everythin'? Fury's got a good master, a good home, an' all the feed he needs to keep him fat an' sassy."

"That's right, he has," Joey agreed.

Pete's happy dream continued, as the pale moonlight crept across the outside of the ranch house and shone through the window upon his smiling face. The old man's grin broadened as he turned the pages of the catalogue and decided to order himself a fifty-dollar pair of handmade boots.

At that moment, his happy dream turned "turrible." Suddenly, he found himself riding a bucking horse before thousands of screaming people. The bawling bronc seemed to be trying to hammer Pete's spine into his neck, as the dust boiled up beneath its thundering hoofs. With one hand Pete got himself a stranglehold on the saddle horn. With the other he grabbed a fistful of the animal's mane. Now the hoofbeats seemed even louder than the clamor of the crowd. As his mount did a corkscrew turn in mid-air, Pete went flying. He landed with a thump and, as he rolled over to avoid being trampled by the pounding hoofs, his head cracked against the leg of the bureau. He woke up yelling, and discovered that, as usual, he had fallen out of bed.

As the angry old man scrambled to his feet, he realized that the sound of hoofbeats was real and not just part of his dream. A horse was galloping down the road toward the ranch gate. With his bare feet slapping the cold floor, he ran to his bedroom door, opened it, and stood blinking as the lights went on in the living room. Jim and Joey were already there in their pajamas. Pete gathered his flapping nightshirt around his spindly legs and scurried toward the hearth, which was still warm from the dying fire.

"What in tarnation's goin' on outside?" he demanded. "What kind of a danged fool'd be ridin' a horse in the middle of the night? An' don't say 'Paul Revere,' 'cause I heerd that joke when I was no bigger'n a hoptoad."

"It's Fury!" Joey cried. "He ran away! I saw him from my window!"

"How'd he git outa the barn?" Pete yelled. "Didn't you bolt the door?"

"Sure I did! But Fury can slide the bolt with his muzzle. You know that!"

"Yeah, I do know it!" Pete shouted sourly. "An' that's what you git fer givin' a horse a trick education! He wakes everybody up at three o'clock in the mornin', when it's cold enough to freeze the snout off a brass hyena."

Jim raised his hand and spoke commandingly. "All right, knock it off, both of you. You sound like a couple of bickering kids."

"But, Jim," Joey said in a despairing voice, "it's Fury! He's gone! What're we going to do?"

"We'll discuss that after we put on bathrobes and slippers. Hurry it up, before we all get pneumonia."

When Jim and Joey returned to the living room, Pete was still standing on the hearth with his back to the poked-up fire. He had tucked up the rear of his nightshirt in order to capture some of the rising heat.

Joey wrinkled his forehead. "Fury hasn't run away from the ranch since I first came here to live. That's when he went out to fight the white stallion. I can't understand why he's done it again tonight."

"Wal, he shore ruined one of my happy dreams," Pete growled, rubbing his head. "An' he raised a lump on my noggin, too." Jim glanced at him and grinned. "Yep," Pete admitted sheepishly, "I fell outa bed agin, dadgum it!"

Jim looked thoughtfully down into the fire. Even in his heavy woolen bathrobe the tall boss of the

Broken Wheel looked vigorous and athletic, and his face beneath the light blond hair was handsome and wind-burned.

"Why do you think Fury ran away, Jim?" Joey asked. "Do you think he went to fight another stallion?"

"I doubt it, Joey. There hasn't been a killer stallion in this region since the white one."

"Yer right," Pete agreed. "If there was, we woulda heerd tell of him long before this."

"Of course," Jim continued, "there are stallions guarding the mares of the mustang herds in the hills, but those aren't killers. Fury wouldn't break out to look for a fight with one of those fellows."

Pete snapped his bony fingers. "The mares! That gives me an idee, Jim. Could be that Fury wants a companion to kinda settle down with."

"That same thought occurred to me," Jim said.

Joey looked at Jim, with disbelief written on his face. "But Fury *has* companions, right here on the ranch. He's got you and Pete and me, and plenty of horses to keep him company."

"That's true, Joey," Jim agreed softly, "but we can't argue with an animal's natural instincts."

"I know that, but golly, I . . ." Joey's voice trailed off as he walked to the window and stared into the night. Jim and Pete exchanged sympathetic glances and waited for him to continue. In a moment Joey turned and spoke in a small, hopeless voice. "I can't believe that Fury'd leave *us* for — well — for *any*thing." He returned to the fireplace and laid his hand on Jim's arm. "Jim, can't we ride out now and bring him back?"

5

"Not in the middle of the night, Joey. It would be a fool's errand."

"Then when?"

"In the morning, right after breakfast."

"Shore," Pete added. "Bein' it's Saturday an' there's no school, the three of us kin ride up together."

Joey gave the mantel an impatient slap. "But suppose Fury's not *in* the hills?"

"He'll be there," Jim assured him. "I'll bet you a new saddle we'll find him with the wild-horse herd." He placed his arm around Joey's shoulder. "Okay son? Satisfied?"

Joey sighed. "I guess so, Jim."

"Good boy. Now let's all try to catch a few hours of shut-eye."

"Smart idee," Pete said. "An' when we git up, I'll build us a breakfast of pork chops an' flapjacks. That'll give our stummicks a little somethin' to work on durin' the ride."

Dejectedly, Joey returned to his room and closed the door.

"You know somethin', Jim?" Pete whispered. "Durned if I don't think that boy's jest plain, downright jealous."

Jim nodded. "I think you're right, but it's understandable. Jealousy's a natural instinct, too."

It was breaking light as the search party rode through the gate of the Broken Wheel and turned into the trail across the meadow that led westward to the high country. Jim took the lead on his bald-faced sorrel; Joey rode second on a calico pony; and Pete brought up the rear on Cactus, his favorite gelding.

At the breakfast table they had discussed their search plans.

"Last week," Jim began, "when I rode up to check the wild herds, the largest one was wintering on Blazing Ridge."

"How many head you figger's in that partic'lar herd?" Pete asked.

"I'd say close to fifty."

"It's been a hard winter. How'd they look?"

"They seemed in pretty good condition. There was one mare among them that I hadn't seen before. She's snow white and a real beauty."

Joey looked up from his plate, frowning. "Do you think that's where Fury went?"

Jim shrugged. "It's a possibility. Anyway, since that herd's on Blazing Ridge, it's the one we'll check first." He pushed his chair back and stood up. "Well, this is one morning we can leave the dishes in the sink. Let's put on our cold-weather gear, saddle up, and get going."

Twenty minutes later they started out. Two-thirds of the way across the meadow trail, they took the left fork and headed for Blazing Ridge. After an hour of riding, as they entered the edge of the forest, Jim raised his hand and turned in his saddle.

"What's up?" Pete called.

Jim pointed as his companions pulled even with him. The timbered bridge that had carried the trail across a wide mountain stream had been washed away. "It must've been that sudden thaw we had last week," Jim said. "Between the ice and the rushing water, the bridge didn't stand a chance."

"Gosh, there's always something," Joey complained. "Here we are, in a hurry to find Fury, and we can't get across the stream."

"That's the way it always is," Pete grumbled. "Nothin' ever comes easy."

Joey brought his mount to the bank of the icy stream, looked down, and called over his shoulder. "Can't we ease our horses down the bank and ride across?"

"We can't ask horses to do that," Jim answered sharply. "That water's below freezing."

"But, Jim, we've got to get up to the ridge."

"That's right, Joey, and we will."

"But how?"

"By using our brains." Jim pointed off to the right. "We'll have to make a long detour in that direction. That way we'll get to the herd without having to cross the stream."

Pete made a wry face. "That means we'll hafta cross Mark Yancey's property."

"That's right. But Mr. Yancey won't mind, once we explain our problem."

"I bet he'll be plenty mad, though," Joey said. "He's a pretty disagreeable character."

Pete nodded. "You kin say that agin. He's the most unfriendly cuss I ever heerd of. A real pain in the collar button."

"Why?" Jim asked. "What did Yancey ever do to you fellows?"

"Well, I don't know about Pete," Joey said, "but

last summer, when Packy and I went camping in the hills, Mr. Yancey chased us away. He was real mean about it, too."

"Were you on his property by any chance?"

"Well, yes," Joey admitted. "But just over the edge."

"In that case he was within his rights." Jim turned to Pete. "Now what did Yancey ever do to you?"

Pete's eyes wavered. "Wal, nothin' that you could rightly put yer finger on. But all the ranchers in the valley tell me he's as mean as a wet polecat."

Jim pushed his hat back with his thumb. "You're certainly a fine pair of character assassins. You've blackened a man's reputation on no evidence at all." He brought his horse around. "Come on. Let's ride up and find out what kind of a man Mr. Yancey really is."

Mark Yancey was a lumberman who had moved from the Northwest several years earlier and bought a large tract of woodland adjacent to Blazing Ridge. Since his arrival, he had carried out logging operations in all seasons of the year. Although a small part of his acreage contained vigorous, productive stands of timber, the greater portion was poorly stocked; and he had made no attempt to put the land back to work by planting new seedlings.

Several well-meaning lumbermen had advised Yancey to replant trees for a future yield, but he had paid no attention to them. In addition, he cut his timber carelessly, with little advance planning. Jim pointed out this obvious fact as the riders skirted the edge of Yancey's timber tract, seeking the road into the property. Hundreds of stumps could be seen among damaged trees.

"Look at those trees with their bark scraped off," Jim said. "That makes them an easy prey to rot."

Pete clucked his tongue. "You kin see Yancey ain't very careful when he's cuttin' his trees."

"Careless falling and tractor operation can ruin a fine, growing forest," Jim added. "A little care would've saved damage to those trees left standing."

"An' lookit them high stumps," Pete said. "Cuttin' trees so high up off the ground is a waste of money an' timber."

From deep in the woods came the shrill screech of a power saw.

"They're working in there," Joey said in surprise. "I didn't know they cut trees in the wintertime."

"Logging can be done all year around," Jim explained. "Of course, it's cheaper in summer than in winter because of the snow problem, but winter logging has a few advantages, too. Machines and manpower are easier to get at this time of year, and the rate of pay is lower."

Pete grunted. "I bet Yancey's a skinflint, too — as well as a pain in the collar button."

Jim shot the rambunctious old man a look, but made no comment.

"Anyway," Joey said, "I just hope Mr. Yancey's seen Fury, that's all I care about."

"If we should bump into Mr. Yancey or any of his men," Jim advised, "you'd better let me do most of the talking."

After another fifteen minutes of silent riding,

they came to a rutted skid trail. Yancey's property on their right was studded with stumps, while the trees on the left were uncut.

"I wonder why Yancey ain't logged that other side," Pete said. "Sech healthy-lookin' trees'd fetch a mighty fancy price at the sawmill."

"He wouldn't dare touch this forest on the left," Jim explained. "It's public-domain land. The trees belong to the United States government."

"What would happen if he did cut them down?" Joey asked.

"He'd be fined and imprisoned. Government timber is under the protection of the Bureau of Land Management. Anyone who cut it would be charged with timber trespass."

"That's right," Pete said. "They call it 'timber rustlin'.' Instead of stealin' horses, they'd be stealin' trees. The Federal foresters an' the FBI'd clap 'em behind bars the minute they found out about it." He turned to Jim. "Matter of fact, I never knowed this here was gov'ment timber. Must be a big temptation to Yancey, havin' all them fine trees right next to his own property."

"There you go again," said Jim, annoyed. "Believing the worst of a man before you've even met him."

The screech of the power saw became louder as they rode forward. In a moment they rounded a bend and came upon the logging operation in full swing. A small donkey engine added to the din. As the riders came into view, the logging crew of four men looked up in surprise. At a hand signal from one of them, the noise ceased. The man who had given the signal threaded his way over the fallen logs and approached the visitors with a stern expression on his face. His chin and cheeks were darkened by a three-day growth of whiskers, and his boots and mackinaw were covered with sawdust.

"Good morning," said Jim pleasantly. "Is Mr. Yancey here?"

"I'm Mark Yancey," the man snapped. "Who're you?"

"We're from the Broken Wheel, a horse ranch down in the valley. My name's Jim Newton." Jim thrust his hand down for a shake, but Yancey paid no attention to it. Jim smiled. "This is Pete Wilkie, my foreman; and the boy is my son, Joey."

Yancey peered at Joey through a pair of bushy eyebrows. "Joey, huh? I've seen you before, haven't I?"

"Yes, sir," Joey answered shyly. "Last summer, when I came up with a friend to camp out. We made a mistake and camped on your property. You chased us off."

Yancey scowled. "Oh yes, now I remember. You were ridin' a black horse."

"That's right," Joey said eagerly. "Fury. That's why we rode up here today, Mr. Yancey, to look . . ."

"We're sorry to interrupt your work, Mr. Yancey," Jim cut in, "but we're trying to get to Blazing Ridge."

"Then why didn't you follow the trail? You're way off base."

"We know that, sir, but the bridge was out. The only way we could get to the ridge was across this property. Would you be kind enough to give us permission?"

"Why? What's so important on the Ridge?"

"A herd of mustangs is wintering up there," Jim explained. "Early this morning Joey's horse, Fury, broke away from the ranch and we think he might've gone to join the herd."

Yancey's eyes showed a flicker of interest. Turning, he addressed one of his men who was shambling toward the group. "Hey, Bud, you hear that?"

"Hear what?" the man asked blankly.

Yancey disregarded the question and spoke to Jim. "This is Bud Snape, my loggin' boss."

Jim gave Snape, a hulking man dressed in work clothes, a polite greeting.

"These riders are from a horse ranch down below," Yancey told Snape. "I bet you can't guess what they're lookin' for."

Snape frowned. "How could I? I'm no mind reader."

"They're lookin' for a black horse that ran off last night."

Snape's broad, flat face lighted up, and he flashed a broken-toothed grin. "No kiddin'," he said. "I'll be doggoned." He looked up at Jim. "So that black critter belonged to you, huh?"

Joey leaned forward eagerly. "You mean you saw Fury?"

Snape wrinkled his forehead. "Saw *what?*"

"Fury. My horse."

Yancey broke in angrily. "Yes. We saw Fury. He raced through these woods like an express train. Knocked over a stack of empty oil drums and woke everybody up."

Pete guffawed. "That's Fury, all right."

Yancey glared at Pete. "It's no laughin' matter. He might've done a lot of damage."

Joey was anxious to get going. "Come on, Jim, let's look for him."

"Easy, Joey, we will," said Jim. He turned to Yancey. "We're sorry that our horse caused you so much trouble. If any damage was done, I'll gladly pay for it."

Snape spoke up. "Don't worry, mister, yer horse didn't bust anythin'. Just made a heck of a racket, that's all. 'Specially when he ran back through here with a white mare."

"A *white* mare?" said Jim. "Are you sure?"

"An' how. That mustang was as white as a ghost."

"Look," Yancey said impatiently, "you're wasting my time. Like Snape said, your horse was running with a white mare. Now ride anywhere you want to ride, but find him in a hurry and clear out."

"Thanks, Mr. Yancey, we'll do that," Jim said pleasantly. He slapped his rein. "Let's ride."

As they left the road and cut into the woods, Snape called after them. "There's a clearin' about a half-mile straight ahead. I betcha ya'll find them two horses grazin' there together."

"Thanks, Bud," Jim called back. "Sounds like a good tip."

"Wal, Jim, what'd I tell you," Pete said, after they had ridden out of earshot. "Is Yancey an unfriendly cuss or ain't he?"

"He is," Jim answered with a chuckle. "And he's also a pain in the collar button."

Joey peered through the trees ahead. "Gosh, I

14

sure hope we find Fury in that clearing. If we don't, we'll have to ride all the way up to Blazing Ridge."

"Simmer down," Jim said. "We'll have Fury back before the day's over."

When the light grew brighter in the dusky forest, Jim gave the hand signal to halt. "The clearing's just ahead. Let's continue as quietly as possible."

In a moment Joey caught his breath and pointed. "There!" he exclaimed in a low voice. "Look!"

Grazing at the far edge of the clearing, gleaming snowy white in the sunlight, was the mustang mare. Fury stood grazing beside her. Hearing the approaching riders, he flung his head up and gave an angry stallion scream. The mare leaped sideways, whinnying in fright.

"Call him, Joey!" Jim commanded. "Let him know it's you!"

"Fury!" Joey shouted. "Fury, it's me!"

Fury bent his ears toward the sound of the voice, then turned to the mare and voiced a shrill command. She wheeled obediently and raced from the clearing into the safety of the forest.

"Come on!" Pete yelled. "Let's catch him before he takes off after her!"

As they burst into the clearing, Fury darted away in the direction taken by the fleeing mare.

"Fury!" cried Joey. "Fury, come back!"

"Dismount!" Jim barked. "Try to coax him back, before he gives us a chase." Jim caught hold of the pony's bridle as Joey leaped to the ground.

Fury had hesitated at the far edge of the clearing. Joey walked toward him, slowly.

"Fury, it's Joey. Come to me . . . *please!*"

The great stallion turned his head uncertainly, caught between his instinct to follow the mare and his love for his young master.

"Lookit him," Pete muttered. "Right now he's half-wild an' half-tame. He kin go either way."

"I think Joey will win," Jim said. "Temporarily, anyway."

The men sat quietly in their saddles, watching the youngster in his struggle to win Fury back. Joey was pleading softly, with both arms outstretched. Ten yards from the trembling stallion he stopped and called Fury's name. He was no longer pleading, he was demanding obedience. Fury looked at the outstretched arms, took a pace forward, then glanced back into the woods. Finally, with a sigh that was almost human, Fury made his decision, cantered to Joey's side, and pushed his muzzle against the boy's shoulder. Joey placed his palm against Fury's soft upper lip and rubbed it lovingly.

"Thanks, Fury," he whispered. "I'm glad you decided to come with me, instead of *her*."

The stallion threw his head back and nickered with delight. Grasping the thick mane, Joey vaulted to his back and rode him across the clearing.

"Good work, Joey," Jim said.

Riding in a circle, to avoid meeting Mr. Yancey again, they made their way back to the skid trail a half-mile below the logging operation. It was high noon as they cantered through the gate of the Broken Wheel.

Chapter 2

A MASCOT FOR FURY

Spring came early to the valley. In April, after winter had retreated for good, the Broken Wheel Ranch hummed with activity. Jim Newton's business was to capture and gentle wild horses, and sell them to cattlemen as working ponies and to rodeos as bucking stock. In preparation for the coming of the new herd of mustangs, Jim and a group of newly hired hands had built several new corrals and stocked the hayloft with feed. When all was ready, the riders set out for the roundup.

Catching the wild horses called for plenty of hard work and hard riding. Corrals were built in selected spots, where the mustangs were watering. The corrals were set up in canyons or deep draws, so that once the horses entered the chutes they found themselves at a dead end, unable to escape. After a day or two in the catch corrals, to get them accustomed to a fence, the animals were herded down to the BW and turned loose in the new enclosures.

Now, once again, Jim Newton was in business. The next step was to break the green broncs to saddle and bridle. When this exhausting work was completed, the new stock was ready for sale.

Jim and Pete had not seen the white mare during the roundup. Jim reasoned that she had either escaped them or run away to join another herd. During the breaking point, Fury was ever on the alert. Standing at the edge of his own corral, with his head held high and his nose searching the air, he seemed to be seeking a sign that the mare was among the newcomers. When it became obvious that she was nowhere in the area, he became nervous and went off his feed.

Joey himself was uneasy during this period. "I had a hard time with Fury on the way home from school," he told Jim one afternoon. "He didn't want to be held down to a canter. All he wanted was to get back to the ranch in a big hurry."

Jim nodded. "I think you'd better keep him in the barn at night, until he settles down. He might get ideas about breaking away again, as he did last February."

"Yeah," said Pete, coming in from the kitchen. "An' put a padlock on the barn door. He's a smart critter, but not smart enough to open a padlock with his nose."

Joey looked out the window toward Fury's corral. "I'm worried about him. Look at him. He's just standing there at the fence, staring at the new horses."

Jim looked out over Joey's shoulder. "We might as well face the fact that he'll never be happy until he has that white mare as a companion."

Joey flushed. "I wish that darn white mare had never been born."

"Well," said Jim, "Fury senses that she's up in the hills somewhere, so it's a problem we can't duck. If he doesn't settle down pretty soon, we'll have to ride up and look for her."

"Jim! You mean you'd bring the mare down here to the ranch?"

"Yep, if we have to. If Fury had the mare to run with in the corral, it wouldn't mean that he'd like you any the less."

"But he's *my* horse!" Joey cried. "I'm the one that broke him, and I'm the only one that can ride him!"

"That's true. And those are the very reasons why you should want him calmed down and happy."

Joey remained silent, but his face was clouded and angry.

Pete spoke up gaily. "Say, Joey, I tell you what. I'll bake one of yer fav'rite pies fer supper — coc'nut custard. That oughta make you git over bein' jealous, huh?"

Joey whirled around. "I'm *not* jealous!"

Pete raised his hand, hastily. "Okay, okay, so yer not. My mistake." He made a low bow. "Pardon me, yer majesty."

"Well, son," said Jim. "Whatever your trouble is, it's not doing you any good. So if we want peace around this ranch we'd better put our heads together and come up with something. What do you suggest?"

19

"I don't know," Joey said gloomily. "I just know that white mare would spoil everything."

"All right, so you have nothing concrete to offer." Jim turned to Pete. "What about you?"

The old foreman rubbed the stubble on his chin. "Wal, I offered a coc'nut custard pie an' got jumped on. I dunno what else to say, 'cept what all three of us know already. Joey's upset 'cause Fury's upset. An' Fury's upset 'cause he's got a hankerin' fer the white mare. Jim, you want the mare here on the ranch, but Joey don't. An' that leaves us settin' in a great big kettle of fish with our boots on."

Jim smothered a grin. "Does that mean you haven't any other suggestions?"

"No, it don't. Matter of fact, I been beatin' my brains out fer the last three days, tryin' to think of somethin'. An' jest now in the kitchen I did think of somethin'."

"You did?" said Joey eagerly. "What is it?"

Pete folded his arms. "Wal, first of all I want you to know I already made that coc'nut custard pie. Are you gonna eat it or ain't you?"

"Sure I am," Joey grinned. "Now tell us what you thought of."

"Wal," the old man began, "I been around horses fer a good many years. All kinds of horses — little runty ones an' high-spirited ones like Fury. An' I happen to know that high-spirited horses're always happier with some kinda animal pal to run around with."

Joey's face fell. "There you go again with the white mare."

"Rest yer tonsils!" Pete said sharply. "The white

20

mare's got nothin' to do with it." He glared at Joey and continued. "Jest the other day I seen in the paper about a champîon race horse that's got a billy goat fer a mascot. Seems like this horse won't even eat or sleep unless the goat's right there in the stall with him."

"That's right," said Jim. "I read that story in the paper."

"Once, down in the Panhandle of Texas," Pete went on, "I knew a stallion that had a hen fer a mascot. Him an' that hen was closer'n five minutes to eleven. He wouldn't even walk into his stall till the old biddy flew up and perched on his back."

Joey smiled. "Are you kidding, Pete? Did you ever really see the hen on the stallion's back?"

"Shore I seen her. Ev'ry mornin', reg'lar as clock-work, she laid a brown egg in his mane. I hadda git up early ev'ry day to rescue the egg afore it got broke." Pete wrinkled his nose. "Ever try to comb a busted egg outa a horse's mane? It's harder'n tryin' to shake a collar button out of a guitar."

Jim spoke up. "Then you're suggesting that Joey should find some kind of an animal mascot for Fury, is that it?"

"Right. A goat, a hen, a cat, a dog, mebbe even a bull-frog fer all I know. Leastways, all Joey kin do is try to find some kinda little critter that Fury might dote on enough to simmer him down."

"What do you think of the idea, Joey?" Jim asked.

"I think it's great — if it works."

"It'll work," Pete assured him. "But on'y if you find the right critter. If I was you, I'd saddle Fury an' start lookin'."

"I'll take him over to Mr. Appleton's farm," Joey said, "and introduce him to Mrs. Appleton's goat. If he likes the goat, maybe I can buy him with the money I've been saving."

"Good idea," said Jim, "but first you've got to go and clean out the stalls."

"Sure, Jim, right away."

After his chore was completed, Joey mounted Fury and rode down the valley to the Appleton farm. Explaining to the astonished Mrs. Appleton his reason for coming, he led Fury by the bridle to the far corner of the barnyard, where he found the goat standing on the roof of the henhouse. The goat took one look at Fury and lowered his horns. Fury took one look at the goat and bent his ears back.

"What's the matter, Fury?" Joey asked. "Don't you like this beautiful goat?"

Fury wiggled his nostrils and turned his head away.

"Gosh, I can't say I blame you," Joey said, trying not to breathe through his nose, "but I just thought you might like him."

Mrs. Appleton came across the yard. "Well, Joey, how'd it go? Do Fury and Billy like each other?"

"Well, yes," Joey fibbed, "but not well enough to live together. Have you got a nice friendly hen that we might try?"

"Oh, I have hundreds of hens. Wait right here and I'll bring one out to you."

When Mrs. Appleton returned with the hen, Joey held it tightly and placed it on Fury's back. Fury bucked and threw his head around. The hen took

22

one look at the wide, frightened eyes, cackled furiously, and gave Joey a nasty peck on the hand.

"Ouch!" Joey yelped. "Here, Mrs. Appleton, please take your hen back. I don't think she'd make a very good mascot for Fury."

"It doesn't seem so, does it?" The kindly woman glanced around the barnyard. "Let's see now. Have you thought of a pig, Joey? I have a very sweet pig that might be just what you and Fury are looking for."

"Well, I've never heard of a horse and a pig being friends, but we can see."

"All right, just follow me. The pigpen's right over here."

"I'm not sure Jim would like having a pig in our barn," Joey said, "but if Fury and the pig spark to each other maybe I can argue Jim into letting it come."

When they arrived at the pen it was plain to see that Fury had no intention of accepting a pig as a mascot. The pig had similar feelings about the scheme, so Joey thanked Mrs. Appleton for her trouble and rode back to the ranch.

"Mebbe Fury'd like some wild animal," Pete said, after Joey had related his disappointing experience. "If I was you, I'd ride into the woods on Saturday. You might find a raccoon or somethin' like that that'd take his fancy."

"I doubt it," Joey said, with a sigh. "But I guess it's worth a try."

When Saturday came, Joey had his usual morning ranch work to do before starting out on any mission of his own. As he was filling the big water trough just outside the barn, a small, covered truck chugged through the ranch gate. Looking up, Joey recognized the wheezing vehicle at once.

"Jim!" he shouted. "Look who's coming! Doc Beemis!"

Jim appeared overhead at the door of the hayloft and waved his arm in greeting. Pete leaned out the kitchen window.

"Wal, I'll be dadgummed," Pete cried. "Where's that ole fraud been all these months?"

As the truck clattered up the rise to the ranch house, Joey could read the lettering on one of the side panels:

THEY WHO SUFFER ACHE AND PAIN
NEED NEVER SUFFER MORE AGAIN!
Dr. Archibald P. Beemis
Surgeon, Pharmacist,
and Friend in Need

Joey had met Doc Beemis the previous summer, when Doc had stopped off at the BW to wash his socks and get rested up before continuing the long trip around his sales territory. Doc — a stout, elderly man with darting eyes, silver hair, and a nose like a red mushroom — drove wherever the roads were passable, peddling patent medicines, nerve tonics, and "sure cures" for coughs, colds, chilblains, and "the heartaches and the thousand natural shocks that flesh is heir to."

Doc Beemis was a throwback to the traveling medicine peddler of the Old West. He had a sure cure for everything, and even though he could talk the hind leg off a donkey, everyone welcomed him because of his geniality and endless store of tall tales.

As the truck crawled up the rise and shuddered to a stop before the ranch house, Jim slid down the feed-loading rope to the ground. Pete hurried from the house, wiping his hands on his apron.

Joey ran to the side of the truck. "Hello, Doc! Gosh, it's great to see you again!"

Doc Beemis leaned out the window and extended his hand. "Joseph, my boy," he said with a nasal twang, "I'm overjoyed to see you. And astonished as well, by the way you've grown since I last stopped at the Broken Wheel."

"Welcome, Doc," Jim said warmly.

"I thank you, James," Doc said, glancing about. "I see you still possess the fairest horse ranch in the Western Hemisphere."

"Cut out the blarney, you ole scoundrel," Pete said, "an' shake hands with the real boss of the BW."

"Peter," said Doc loftily, "I'll thank you to address me with a pinch of politeness and a modicum of decorum befitting my high professional status."

"Bushwa!" Pete said. "Climb down outa that rattletrap an' stretch yer drumsticks."

As Doc opened the door, something resembling a large ball of dirty wool leaped from the interior of the truck onto the front seat.

Pete jumped back, startled. "What the Sam Hill's that thing?"

"This is man's best friend," Doc announced proudly.

Pete raised his eyebrows. "A dog?"

"Precisely. He is my companion, comforter, and canine friend. A noble descendant, in unbroken line,

25

from the wild wolf of the lonely prairies. His name is Crosby."

Joey laughed. "Crosby? That's a funny name for a dog. Why do you call him Crosby?"

"Because he sings so beautifully," Doc explained. "Listen carefully. He'll give you a concert." He turned to the dog. "Sing, Crosby!" Doc commanded.

The dog threw his head back and emitted a series of mournful howls.

"Ah," Doc said, smiling, "isn't that delightful? Have you ever heard such perfect pitch, such pear-shaped tones?"

"He sounds like a rusty hinge that needs oil," Pete said flatly.

"I think he's just great," Joey said.

As Doc Beemis climbed down from the truck, Crosby leaped from the seat and ran in happy circles. His black, beady eyes were almost covered by shaggy hair; his paws were enormous, and his tail was a tuft of wagging fur. One white ear stood up straight, and the other ear, which was brown, lay flat. When he had finished running, he bounded toward Joey, placed his giant paws on Joey's shoulders, and licked his face with a long pink tongue.

"Crosby finds you delicious, Joseph," Doc said.

Jim and Pete laughed, as Joey wrestled with the tremendous dog.

"How long can you stay with us, Doc?" Jim asked.

"Overnight, James," said Doc, "if you don't mind."

"Fine. Stay as long as you like."

"That's kind of you, but I must get started early in

the morning. Meanwhile, perhaps Peter will treat me to one of his magnificent meals, possibly two or three."

"I shore will," Pete said. "What'd you eat fer supper last night?"

Doc's eyes twinkled. "A thousand things — beans."

"In that case we won't have beans fer dinner," Pete promised. "I'll barbecue a mess of spareribs. An' fer dessert, how about a nice dish of tapioca?"

Doc wrinkled his red nose. "Tapioca? Not for me, my friend. I'd rather ride into a west wind with a funnel in my mouth."

Pete chuckled. "Okay, you big lummox. We'll have chocolate ice cream instead. An' I'll cook us a big pot of my famous coffee."

"Ah, sounds excellent. Are you brewing coffee in your usual way?"

"That's right, I still use the ole cowboy recipe: Take one pound of coffee, wet it good with water, boil it over a hot fire fer thirty minutes, pitch a horseshoe in it, an' if it sinks, throw in some more coffee."

"Magnificent!" Doc said. "And one tiny spoonful of sugar, if you please."

"Go inside and make yourself at home," said Jim. "Meantime, we'll finish our morning chores."

"Wait a second," Joey said. "Let's see if I can get Crosby to sing for me." He pushed the dog away and held him at arm's length. "Sing, Crosby!" he ordered.

The shaggy dog made a few squeaks to warm up, then took a deep breath, and howled as before. From Fury's corral came an answering whinny.

Everyone laughed but Doc Beemis. "Bless my soul!" he exclaimed. "What in the world was that sound?"

"That was Fury," Joey said. "I guess he liked Crosby's voice."

"Ah yes, Fury. A sensible horse, that stallion of yours. He appreciates fine music."

Joey stayed outside with Crosby, who drank thirstily from the water trough. Fury had come to the near fence of his corral, and seemed to be watching the dog with great interest.

"Come on, Crosby," Joey said. "I'll take you over and introduce you to Fury."

The dog bounded gaily at Joey's side. As they arrived at the corral, Fury bent his ears forward and leaned over the fence. Crosby made happy dog noises and rubbed his nose against Fury's muzzle. Fury stepped back and cantered around the corral. Crosby, wriggling with joy, squeezed through the bars of the fence and ran beside him, leaping up playfully. Fury seemed pleased with his new friend. For a moment Joey watched them playing like a colt and a puppy, then raced back to the barn.

"Jim!" he shouted. "Fury's found a mascot! Look at them out there!"

Jim shaded his eyes and watched the two animals chasing each other around the enclosure.

"They're certainly having a fine time. Fury's acting like a youngster."

"They took to each other right away," Joey said excitedly. "Jim, do you think we can have Crosby? He'll make Fury forget that white mare in no time."

"You may be right, but don't get your hopes up before you ask Doc Beemis. Maybe Doc doesn't want to part with him."

"I'll ask him. I'll tell him I'll buy Crosby — for cash."

"Go to it," Jim said. "And good luck."

Doc Beemis was shaving in Pete's bathroom when Joey ran in. Startled, Doc nicked his chin with the razor.

"Drat!" he exclaimed. "Don't *ever* sneak up behind a man when he's using a straight razor. You almost made me slice my jugular vein."

"I'm sorry," Joey said breathlessly, "but this is important. It's about Crosby."

Doc's jaws dropped. "Good grief! Don't tell me my dog has eaten one of the horses!"

"No. He loves horses, especially Fury."

Joey told Doc about Fury's need of a mascot, and finished by asking if he'd consider selling Crosby. The man seemed shocked at the idea.

"What? Do you have the audacity to suggest that I would part with my shaggy partner for mere gold?"

Joey hesitated. "Well, I know how you feel about Crosby. I'm sure you love him very much. But Fury loves him, too, and he loves Fury. So please, Doc, won't you let me buy him?"

Doc Beemis dabbed at the cut on his chin before answering. "Joseph, my lad," he said finally, "obviously you don't realize the value of that noble animal. Crosby is descended from a long line of canine kings, beginning with a royal creature named Tomarctus, who roamed the world fifteen million years before you were born."

"No kidding," said Joey, amazed. "Is that the truth?"

"Naturally. I wouldn't delude you for all the gold in the world. Do you honestly think you can afford to purchase such a priceless treasure?"

"Gosh, I guess not," answered Joey glumly. "I had no idea Crosby was such a great dog." He turned to leave. "Thanks, anyway."

"Wait," said Doc. "Don't give up so easily. Even though Crosby is my four-footed companion of the open road, I wouldn't stand in the way of his finding a good home, that is, if the price is right. What figure did you have in mind?"

Joey saw a ray of hope. "Well, I have ten dollars and forty-eight cents. Would that be enough?"

Doc thought for a moment. "You have that amount in cash?"

"Sure, I was saving up for a new saddle."

Doc's eyes glistened with sentiment. "It touches my heart, Joseph, that you would sacrifice a new saddle for a mere dog."

"What do you mean a 'mere' dog? You just told me Crosby was a priceless treasure."

"That's true," Doc said quickly, "I did, and it's a fact. But there's something about a boy yearning for a dog that twangs the strings of my heart. What was the exact amount you offered?"

"Ten dollars and forty-eight cents."

"It's a deal. Crosby's yours."

"Oh boy!" cried Joey, grabbing Doc's arm.

"Drat!" said Doc. "*Never* seize a man's arm when he's holding a blade against his throat!"

"I'm sorry," Joey said, running out of the bathroom. "Wait'll I tell Jim and Pete I've got a mascot for Fury!"

During the rest of the morning it was evident that Fury and Crosby were made for each other. The playful, shambling dog refused to leave Fury's side, even when called to the house for lunch. In the end, Joey was obliged to carry a large plateful of food out to the corral, which he did happily.

"How do you like him, Fury?" Joey asked. "Isn't he the greatest?"

Fury poked Crosby with his nose, then raised his head and gave a satisfied snort. Crosby answered by breaking into one of his mournful songs.

"I don't think you'll have to lock Fury in the barn anymore at night," said Jim at suppertime. "He'll never run away as long as Crosby's close by."

Joey grinned. "Boy, I'm sure glad we got that settled. I was really worried."

"Go on," Pete said. "You wasn't worried — you was plumb jealous. Come on now, Joey, admit it. Wasn't you jealous?"

"Sure I was," Joey confessed.

Doc Beemis leaned across the table and helped himself to a heaping spoonful of mashed potatoes. "Then why aren't you jealous of Crosby? He and Fury are thick as two thieves."

"I know, but I don't mind his liking a dog. A mare's different."

After supper, when Joey went to the corral with a basinful of bones for Crosby, he found Fury and the dog still frisking together. As Crosby tackled the bones, Fury sidled up to Joey and nuzzled his cheek.

"Thanks," Joey said. "I'm glad you still like me, too."

Fury made a loving sound, deep down in his throat.

Back in the kitchen, while the men were "manicurin' the goldern dishes," as Pete put it, Jim asked Doc Beemis his plans for the summer.

"I'll be touring the glorious West," Doc answered, "selling my wares as usual. But as I travel, I plan to keep my eyes open for something I've been seeking for the past two years."

"I kin guess what that'd be," said Pete, with a chuckle. "A rich millionaire that you kin sell a truckload of them phony medicines to."

Doc looked hurt. "I resent that remark. This year I'm offering a remarkable medical discovery called Swain's Ointment, which will be a blessing to man, woman, and child."

"Shore," Pete scoffed, "as long as they don't drink it."

Jim was interested in Doc's plan. "What is it you're looking for?"

"A wife," Doc said, gazing into space.

Pete howled with glee. "A wife? Now who in tarnation'd marry an old codger like you?"

"Scoff if you will, Peter, but it's true. The time has come for me to cease wandering hither and yon. So what I seek now is a sensible woman who will comfort me in my declining years."

"That's great news," Jim said. "I certainly hope you find her."

"Thank you, James." Doc lowered his voice. "By the way, where's Joseph?"

"Out at the corral with Fury and Crosby."

"Good," said Doc, reaching into his pocket. "In the morning, after I've departed, I'd like you to give him this money." He handed Jim ten dollars and forty-eight cents. "It's the sum he paid for that flea-bitten mongrel of mine."

"I don't get it. Why should you return his money? He made a business deal with you."

"True, but he got the worst of it. To be honest with you, that dog's howling has driven me close to the looney-bin. In fact, I would have *paid* the boy ten dollars and forty-eight cents to take the miserable mutt off my hands."

"Okay," Jim said. "Joey'll be mighty happy to have both the dog and the money."

"He shore will," agreed Pete. He lay a hand on Doc's shoulder. "We're gonna miss you, you ole coot. When do you figger on drivin' back this way?"

"In October — about six months from now — unless I find the woman of my dreams. In that happy event I'll send you a wedding announcement."

Early the next morning, when Doc Beemis drove away, Crosby didn't even look up. He was too busy romping with Fury.

Chapter 3
PACKY COMES HOME

In mid-June, on the last day of school, Joey said good-bye to Miss Miller, his teacher, and walked to the grove where Fury and the other horses were tethered. Crosby, who had been sniffing at an anthill, yelped with joy and ran forward to meet Joey.

Since his arrival at the Broken Wheel in April, the shaggy dog had accompanied Joey and Fury to school each day. The children were delighted with him and often played with him during recess and lunch periods. Miss Miller, however, although fond of Crosby, found him a bit of a nuisance, especially when he'd break into song outside the classroom window while she was trying to teach her pupils long division.

"Crosby's a splendid dog," she said to Joey one afternoon, "but can't you teach him not to howl?"

"Gosh, Miss Miller, I don't think so. Besides, it isn't really howling, it's singing."

The teacher smiled. "I hardly think his namesake would call it singing. Anyway, I hope you'll try to teach him not to use so much volume."

"Okay, Miss Miller, I'll see what I can do."

But despite Joey's attempts, Crosby never learned to lower his voice.

When school closed for the summer, Miss Miller heaved a sigh of relief as Joey and his animals started homeward.

Back at the Broken Wheel, Joey was pleased to find a letter from his young friend Packy Lambert, whom he hadn't seen for almost a year. The Lamberts owned a small ranch a few miles up the valley. When Packy's father had accepted an offer of an important position in California, he had closed his ranch temporarily and taken his family further west. Before leaving, Packy asked Jim Newton to board his horse, Lucky, until he returned, and Jim had been happy to do so.

Packy's letter was full of good news. He and his parents planned to return to their valley home early in August.

"That'll be fine," Jim said. "Chris and Stella Lambert are good neighbors, and Packy's a great little guy."

"He sure is," Joey agreed. "He says here he wants me to teach him to rope this summer. That'll be fun. Oh, and he wants to know how Lucky's getting along. Listen to what he wrote: 'Please tell Lucky I can't hardly wait to ride him again, and next time you go to the barn please give him a kiss for me on his fat little nose. P.S. Say hi to Fury and Jim and Pete. Your friend Packy.'"

"It'll be nice to see that happy little critter agin," Pete said. "Packy's jest about the nicest friend you got."

"You said it. He's five years younger than me, but we get along fine."

Pete grinned. "I wonder how he'll git along with Crosby. Him an' that dog are jest about the same size."

"I bet Packy'll like him a lot. He's always wanted a dog anyway, so we ought to have a lot of fun together this summer. Especially when we go camping overnight."

"Wal, you better not camp on Mark Yancey's property agin," Pete warned. "Crosby might start singin' in the middle of the night an' drive him crazy."

"We won't go anywhere near Mr. Yancey's place, you can bet. He scares me."

"He spooks me, too. I don't want no part of that feller."

Joey folded Packy's letter and put it in his pocket. "Gosh, I miss Packy, you know it? I sure wish it was August instead of June."

"August will be here before you know it," Jim said. "Meanwhile, let's take care of the ranch and enjoy ourselves as much as possible."

"That's the spirit," said Pete. "An' the way things've been goin', we got a lot to be thankful fer. Back in February we thought we was gonna have trouble with Fury. But since he's got Crosby fer a mascot, everythin's hunky-dory."

Joey looked out toward the corral. Crosby was

curled up on the ground, fast asleep in Fury's shadow.

"I think Fury's forgotten all about that white mare, don't you, Jim?"

Jim looked up from a letter he'd been reading. "Hm? Sorry, Joey, I didn't hear you."

"The white mare. Don't you think Fury's forgotten all about her?"

"It looks that way." Jim put his letter aside and consulted the wall calendar.

"What's that letter?" Pete asked. "You been readin' it over an' over, ever since it come."

"Nothing to get worked up about," Jim assured him.

"Wal, that's good." Pete joined Joey at the window. "I feel the way you do, Joey, about that mare, 'cause this here's a man's ranch. Even Crosby's a he-male. We got mares an' fillies here, shore, but they don't do no harm, 'cause they come an' go. But if Fury's white lady was here there'd be trouble, as shore as shootin'."

"I guess there would, Pete."

"It don't make no dif'rence whether it's a human bein' or an animal," Pete went on vehemently. "Females always make trouble, 'specially on a ranch."

"And how!" said Joey.

Jim's stern voice brought their heads around. "Now look, fellows, you'd better change your tune about females on a ranch, because I've got news for you."

Pete glanced at the letter in Jim's hand. "What're you talkin' about? Is that letter from a *gal?*"

"Nope, a woman. My Aunt Maggie."

The old man grinned. "Say, how is your ole Aunt Maggie, anyway? She still writin' you advice on how to run a horse ranch?"

"No, there's no advice in this letter."

"Who's Aunt Maggie?" asked Joey. "I never even heard of her." .

"She's an' ole busybody," said Pete.

"Don't listen to him," Jim said. "Aunt Maggie's my father's unmarried sister. I haven't seen her since I was East in the Air Force, but she writes to me regularly. She's a very nice woman, thoughtful and sensible. And Pete doesn't know a blessed thing about her, because he's never even met her."

"But you've let me read some of her letters," Pete argued. "An' she writes to you like you was still a kid in knee britches."

"Anyhow," Jim announced quietly, "Aunt Maggie's coming here for a visit."

Pete smacked his forehead. "Oh *no!*"

Jim nodded. "It's true. She'll be here sometime in August."

"Fer how long?"

"She doesn't say, exactly. Her letter just says 'I'll stay for a few weeks.'"

Joey had been listening attentively. "Where does she live now, Jim?"

"In Philadelphia."

"Boy, that's some distance to travel. Do you think she'll like it here?"

"Certainly. She'll take to ranch life very easily."

Pete glanced up. "Who says so?"

"I do. She was brought up in Kentucky. Her father was a horse trainer."

"Uh-oh, that's bad news. Now she *will* tell us how to run a horse ranch."

Jim grinned. "Good. Maybe you'll learn something."

"Bushwa! The day I hafta learn about horses from a female, that's the day I'll be elected president of the U.S.A.!"

Pete turned on his heel, stomped angrily to his room, and slammed the door.

The weeks rushed by and, as Jim had predicted, August came before they knew it. Pete had never mentioned Aunt Maggie again. But in a later letter she wrote Jim that she planned to arrive on the fifteenth.

Joey was intensely curious about Aunt Maggie and actually looked forward to her visit, although he never mentioned it to Pete. A few times, when Jim and Joey had been working or riding together, Joey had asked questions about Jim's aunt and was convinced that she was not as bad as Pete had painted her.

On the second day of August, Packy Lambert and his parents returned from California. Even before their station wagon was unloaded, Packy jumped on his bike and raced over to the Broken Wheel. After saying hello to everybody, he went to the barn with Joey to see his horse, Lucky. The trim little pony greeted him with a happy whinny.

"Gosh, Lucky, I sure missed you something awful,"

Packy said, reaching up to throw his arms around the pony's neck. "I was scared you'd forget me."

Joey laughed. "Are you crazy? Lucky wouldn't forget you any more than Fury'd forget me."

"I know, but I was away a real long time. I was even going to send him a post card once, but then I remembered he couldn't read."

"You should've sent it anyway. I would've read it to him."

"Give me a boost," Packy said. "I want to sit on his back."

Joey laced his fingers for Packy's foot. "Boy, you're a lot heavier than you were last year."

Packy looked down proudly. "Sure. I gained six pounds and two inches." He scratched Lucky's ears. "Gee, Lucky, you're just about the greatest horse in the whole world."

"No he isn't," Joey said. "Fury's the greatest."

"I guess you're right. Hey, how is Fury, anyway?"

"Fine. He's got a mascot now. Wait'll you see him."

Packy frowned. "A mascot? What's that?"

"Well, kind of a friend."

"A boy?"

"No, dopey, a dog."

"What's his name?"

"Crosby. He's terrific."

Packy looked wistful. "Gee, I sure wish I had a dog. I always wanted one."

"Well, don't get ideas about Crosby. He belongs to Fury. They never leave each other alone for a minute."

Joey told Packy all about his trouble with Fury

and the white mare. Packy's eyes bulged when he heard about the meeting with Mr. Yancey.

"But it's all settled now," Joey said, at the end of the story. "With Crosby for a mascot, Fury'll never run away again."

"When can I see Crosby?" Packy asked.

"Right now. Hop off and I'll take you over to the corral and introduce you."

Packy slid to the floor.

"Don't you think Crosby's a funny name for a dog?" Joey asked, as they headed down the road.

"What's funny about it? I think it's a terrific name for a dog."

"I guess you're right. Matter of fact, I can't imagine him having any other name."

As the boys approached the corral, Fury pranced over to meet them.

"Hi, Fury," Packy said. "Boy, you sure are a wonderful hunk of horse."

As Packy reached up to pat Fury's muzzle, a huge ball of fur struck him in the back and knocked him to the ground. In terror, Packy rolled over and looked up into a round, hairy face.

"What's that?" he yelped. "What *is* it?"

"Crosby," Joey said, doubled up with laughter. "He's playing."

Before Packy could scramble to his feet, the happy dog squatted on his chest and licked his face from ear to ear.

"Hey, cut it out!" Packy cried. "Quit licking me! Joey, get him off me!"

Joey grabbed the wriggling dog by the scruff of the neck and held him off just long enough for Packy to regain his feet. But Crosby broke away and placed his paws on Packy's shoulders, this time bowling him over backward.

"What's the matter with this dog?" Packy yelled. "Is he nutty or something?"

"Sure he's nutty, but he likes you. He wants to rassle."

Packy grinned. "Okay then, we'll rassle."

Laughing, the small boy wrapped his arms around the dog's middle and brought him to the ground. As they rolled over and over in a squirming mass, Fury cocked his ears forward and watched them, wide-eyed. Hearing Crosby barking and growling with delight, he stomped the ground with his left forefoot.

"Hey, Fury, take it easy," Joey said. "Don't get excited; they're only playing."

Fury paid no attention to Joey. As the wrestling match continued, he rolled his eyes upward until Joey could see the whites.

"That's enough, Packy!" Joey shouted. "You better quit."

"What for? We're having fun."

"I know, but Fury's getting spooked. It must be all the hollering and barking." Joey ran to the wrestlers and pulled them apart. "We'd better go up to the house and let him simmer down."

Crosby was leaping at Packy, as if daring him to continue the struggle.

"I'll beat you next time, you old son of a gun!" Packy cried. "You're heavier than me, but I'll beat you. I'll pin your old back right flat on the ground."

Realizing that the roughhouse was over, Crosby spread out on his stomach with his tongue hanging out. With his mouth wide open he seemed to be laughing.

Joey took Packy by the arm. "Come on. We'll go up and get a couple bottles of lemon soda."

"Okay. Can we take Crosby with us?"

"He won't come. He never leaves Fury, no matter what."

"Gosh, I wish he would. I like him."

Fury was still prancing nervously inside the fence.

"Settle down!" Joey called sternly. "Everything's going to be okay."

The boys started up to the house, but when they had taken only a few steps they heard a padding sound behind them. Turning, they saw that they were being followed by Crosby.

"Hey," said Packy, "I thought you said he never leaves Fury."

"He doesn't," answered Joey, frowning. "At least he never has, until this minute." He motioned Crosby away. "Go on, get out of here! Get back to Fury!"

Crosby ducked away from Joey's arm and padded around to Packy's side.

"Look at him," said Packy, laughing. "He's following me."

"Pay no attention to him. He'll go back to Fury in a minute."

But Crosby didn't go back to Fury. He bounced along beside Packy until the boys entered the house and closed the door.

"What's that scratchin' sound I hear?" Pete asked, when they were getting their sodas from the refrigerator.

"It's Crosby," Joey said. "He's on the front porch and wants to get in."

Pete scowled. "That means Fury must be on the front porch, too. Jim won't like that a bit."

"No, Fury's in his corral," said Packy. "Crosby followed me, and was pretty mad when Joey wouldn't let him in the house."

Pete placed his hands on his hips. "You mean to tell me that dog left Fury fer *you?*"

"That's right," Packy answered proudly. "He likes me even better than he likes Fury."

"Wal, fry my hide," Pete muttered. "I never woulda believed it in a million years."

When Jim came around the corner of the house from the south pasture, he couldn't believe it either. "Stop scratching the door!" he said sharply to Crosby. "It's just been painted. Stop it, I said!"

Disregarding the command, the excited dog backed up and threw his weight against the door. Annoyed, Jim picked him up and carried him down to Fury's corral.

"Here, Fury," he said, boosting the squirming dog over the fence. "I don't know why your pal left you, but I'm bringing him back."

Fury made a happy sound and poked Crosby with his muzzle. The dog leaped aside, squeezed through the fence rails, and made a beeline back to the house. Jim returned to the porch, took down a coil of rope, and tied Crosby to the railing. The dog snapped angrily at the rope, then sat down and howled.

When Jim came into the kitchen the boys explained what had happened when Packy appeared at the corral.

"Fury was really mad," Joey said, "when he saw Packy and Crosby rassling. I don't understand it."

"Wal, I do," Pete said. "He's jealous of Packy, that's about the size of it."

"I believe you're right," said Jim. "He's had Crosby all to himself for a long time now, and he resents the dog's attentions to Packy."

"Gee," Packy said in a small voice, "I didn't mean to make trouble. I didn't even see Crosby till he jumped me from behind."

Jim patted him on the head. "We know it isn't your fault, son. There's just something about you that Crosby likes."

"Mebbe it's 'cause the two of them are about the same size," Pete suggested. "I reckon mebbe that flea-bitten scoundrel took one look at Packy and says to hisself, 'Here's somebody I kin rassle without bein' beat.'"

Joey was worried about the sudden turn of events. "What can we do, Jim? Fury might run away again, if Crosby deserts him."

"That's possible, but perhaps Crosby will forget about Packy, once he's off the ranch." Jim turned to Packy. "I hate to do this to you on your first day back, but why don't you go home now and let us see if Crosby will settle down? When you come back tomorrow, maybe everything will be all right."

"Well, okay," Packy said, with a trace of disappointment. "I guess my dad needs me to help him, anyway."

"Come on," said Joey. "I'll help you saddle Lucky and you can ride him back to your place. You can get your bike some other time."

As Packy rode through the ranch gate, Crosby followed him with his eyes and howled. A moment later he gnawed the rope in two and raced down the road.

Packy had ridden less than a quarter of a mile when he heard the dog barking. Turning in his saddle, he saw Crosby racing toward him in a cloud of dust.

"Doggone it," he muttered, although secretly pleased, "now I've got to turn around and lead him back to the ranch."

When Packy arrived at the porch, with Crosby leaping at Lucky's heels, Jim realized he'd have to take some drastic action.

"I'll lock the dog in the tool shed," he told Packy, "until you've had time to get home."

"Okay, Jim. But it wasn't my fault he followed me, honest. I didn't whistle for him or anything."

"We know that, Packy." Jim captured the frisky dog and started toward the tool shed. "Now get going," he called back, "before this bundle of lightning bites my head off."

For a solid hour after the boy had ridden away, Crosby's mournful crooning could be heard from the shed. Fury added to the din by neighing shrilly. Then, all at once, the howling stopped.

"Wal, that's a blessin'," Pete said. "That dadgum racket was drivin' me clean outa my mind."

Joey went to the window. "Do you suppose he's asleep?"

46

"I shore hope so."

As Joey looked out he saw Crosby's rear end just disappearing through the gate at the bottom of the road.

"Hey!" he cried. "He got out! He escaped!"

"Let him go," Jim said. "He'll either find his way to Packy's house or he won't. There's nothing for us to do but wait and see."

During the remainder of the afternoon Fury raced wildly around the corral. Between chores, Jim, Joey, and Pete took turns trying to gentle him down, but were unable to make him listen to reason.

Just as Pete was putting supper on the table the telephone rang. The caller was Chris Lambert, Packy's father. After he and Jim had exchanged greetings, he reported that Crosby had just that minute arrived at the Lamberts.

"Packy told us the whole story," said Chris, "and we understand how much you need the dog. I'll put him in the station wagon and bring him back to you in about an hour."

"No, I'll drive to your place," Jim said, "and save you the trip."

"It's no trouble, Jim. Matter of fact, Stella and I had planned to drop over this evening anyway. It's been a long time since we've all seen each other."

When the Lamberts' station wagon rolled through the gate, Fury whinnied and followed it up the side of his corral until he was stopped by the fence. Crosby gave him one scornful bark and crawled onto Packy's lap.

After the adults had gone inside, the boys took Crosby into the field behind the house, so that Fury wouldn't see him and begin acting up again. Although the dog stayed close to Packy, he was not quite as frisky as he had been during the afternoon.

"I guess he's pooped," Packy said. "He sure must've had a long walk, trying to find my house."

"His tongue's hanging out a mile," Joey said. "I hope he's tired enough to go back to Fury's corral tonight and sleep for about a week."

When the Lamberts were ready to leave, Crosby saw Jim coming toward him with a tie rope and cut around the barn toward the road.

"Well, that's that," Jim said. "He's too smart to let me tie him up again. You folks had better drive along home and let us do the worrying."

About an hour later the phone rang. It was Chris Lambert again, telling Jim that Crosby had just checked in, completely exhausted.

"Well, Chris, it looks as though Fury's lost a mascot," Jim said. "But we'll give it one more try. I'll drive over in the morning and bring him back. Then, if he won't stay put at the BW, we'll have to call it quits."

Twice the following day Crosby was driven back to the ranch, and twice he returned on foot to Packy's house.

"Okay, Chris," said Jim on the phone, "we give up. Tell Packy he's got a dog for keeps."

For several days following the loss of his mascot, Fury sulked in his enclosure and refused to eat. At the end of the second day, as a bracing wind blew eastward from the highlands, he raised his head and searched the air with his trembling nose. After the last light had gone out in the ranch house that night,

Fury made one swift circuit of the corral, then darted forward and cleared the topmost rail of the fence.

A moment later, with the soft sweet grass of the meadow beneath his flying hoofs, Fury was racing westward through the darkness toward the shadowy hills.

Chapter 4

A TERRIBLE SECRET

The calico pony was glistening with sweat as Joey rode him along the narrow trail at the top of Blazing Ridge. Crouching low to avoid being swept from the saddle by the overhanging boughs, Joey examined the forest floor for traces of the mustang herds. Finding no fresh indications that the wild horses had passed that way, he realized that he had climbed too high in his frantic search for Fury. Although he hated to admit the fact, he knew that in order to find his stallion he would first have to locate the white mare.

He had been riding since daylight, when Pete had discovered Fury's absence. The old man's shouts had awakened him, and the sight of the empty corral had brought back the feeling of jealousy. Jim hurried from the house, climbed the fence, and examined the ground.

"There are deep indentations here," he called back. "This is where he took off to clear the fence."

"Gol ding it!" Pete growled. "This would hafta happen on the busiest day of the week. We got a million things to do, an' not enough time to do half of 'em."

"Jim," Joey asked, "how soon can we get started?"

"I'm sorry, Joey, but Pete and I can't possibly ride out today."

Joey looked up in dismay. "Why not?"

"Because Mr. Parker's coming to pick up twelve head of horses. His van will be rolling in here in about an hour and a half."

Joey tried desperately to control a feeling of panic. "But we've got to find Fury and bring him back."

"We all know that, son, but running a ranch is like running any other kind of business. Before we attend to private matters, we must meet our obligations to our customers."

"But can't you go after Mr. Parker picks up his horses?"

"No, because Pete and I are going into town with him, to help him load them at the railroad siding."

"That's a fact," Pete added. "An' while that job's bein' done, I got to see about gittin' the feed onto the cars."

Joey looked out toward the mountains. Jim and Pete exchanged troubled glances. Pete pointed to Joey, then to the mountains, and raised his eyebrows questioningly. Jim thought a moment, then nodded, and spoke to Joey.

"How would you feel about riding up there alone?"

Joey whirled around. "You mean it? You think I could find him by myself?"

"You could certainly try."

" 'Tain't a question of yer gittin' lost or nothin' like that," said Pete. "Gosh knows you've camped up there enough times. An' you've rode up there when you was a Junior Fire Warden. The hard part'll be to locate Fury without help." He shaded his eyes and looked westward. "There's a heck of a lotta open space up there, an' Fury could be in any part of it."

"I'll find him," Joey said. "I'll find him if I have to ride for a week."

Jim clapped him on the back. "Good boy. Now come into the house and study the map. I'll show you where the herds are most likely to be found at this time of the year."

Within a half-hour Joey was in the saddle. Later, the sun was hot on his back as he crossed the bridge that had been repaired after its destruction the winter before. Riding steadily upward, searching carefully for signs of the wild horses, he came finally to the Blazing Ridge trail, and followed it as it threaded its way through the dense timber. A few miles to the north the trail started downward, and the going was easier for the calico pony.

Coming into a stand of ancient pines, in a dark, pungent corridor seldom reached by the sun, Joey spied a white object on the trunk of a tree. Stopping beside it, he saw that it was an official notice proclaiming the timber tract to be the property of the United States government, and warning that private logging was forbidden.

Riding further, he realized that he was crossing the public-domain land that adjoined Mark Yancey's property. It was an unpleasant discovery, for he had no desire ever to see Mr. Yancey again. But he knew that if he were to make a thorough search for Fury, he would be forced to ask the man for permission to ride through his private acreage.

While he was considering what he would say to Mr. Yancey, the pony pricked up its ears, and Joey felt a shudder pass through its body. Thinking that a bear might be close by, his hand went quickly to the stock of his rifle. He brought his mount to a halt, and listened attentively for sounds of crackling in the underbrush. From far off came the screech of a power saw cutting through green timber.

"Gosh," Joey murmured, primarily to hear the sound of a human voice, "I had no idea I was this close to Mr. Yancey's property."

Dreading his certain meeting with the lumberman, he slapped the rein and continued on. As he came closer to the logging operation, the noise increased. He heard the puffing of a donkey engine, the thuds of rolling logs, and presently, the raucous shouts of the lumberjacks.

"I just can't be this close to Mr. Yancey's," he said aloud.

He stiffened as he saw movement among the trees just ahead. Logs were being hauled up by a frame loader, which lifted them with iron hooks and dumped them onto a truck. A short distance away a loading dock was in operation. A rollway had been built, and men using peaveys — heavy wooden levers with pointed metal tips ending in hinged hooks — were rolling small sawed logs onto a second truck. Yancey's logging boss, Bud Snape, was waving his arms and shouting commands. Mr. Yancey himself was not in the group.

The power saw screeched again, its teeth biting into the base of a giant pine. The tree spun as it crashed to the ground, and Joey glimpsed a white square attached to its trunk. And now he realized with horror that Yancey's men were cutting trees that were government property.

When the pine fell, the startled pony gave a loud whinny. All work stopped suddenly, as the loggers turned their heads toward the sound. A few of them dropped their tools and disappeared into the forest.

Snape picked up an axe and squinted in Joey's direction. "Who is it?" he called gruffly. "Who's out there?"

Joey felt his heart pounding. "It's me, Joey Newton."

The pony moved into the work area, carefully avoiding the stumps and stepping gingerly over the felled trees. Snape studied the boy carefully for a moment, then his flat face broke into a relieved grin.

"Well, I'll be jiggered," he boomed. "You're the kid from the horse ranch."

"That's right, the Broken Wheel."

Joey glanced down at the government notice attached to the fallen pine.

"What're you lookin' at?" Snape asked, almost casually.

Joey swallowed hard. "Nothing." He hadn't meant to look at the notice, but the temptation to make sure that it was a government warning was too great to resist.

Snape took hold of the pony's bridle. "Tell me somethin', kid. You can read, can't you?"

"Sure."

"And you seen maybe a couple more of these here signs back there in the woods?"

"Yes, sir, I did."

Snape sighed and ran his fingers through his greasy hair. "Well, in that case me and you'd best walk over to the house and see the boss."

Joey was terrified. "You mean Mr. Yancey?"

"Sure, he's the boss. Come on."

"Wait a second," Joey said. "I don't think I really have to see Mr. Yancey."

"Maybe not, but I got a hunch he's got to see you." Snape looked into the woods. "Hey, did you come up here alone or are those two men with you? I mean the young guy and the old one."

"No, I came by myself."

"What for? You lookin' for that black horse again?"

"Yes," said Joey eagerly. "He broke out last night. Have you seen him?"

Snape opened his mouth to answer, then changed his mind. "Come on, we're goin' to Yancey's."

The members of the logging crew who hadn't run away had been listening in silence.

"What're you jacks standin' around for?" Snape bawled at them. "Jump to it! Get them sticks down and loaded!"

As the men returned to work, Snape led the pony by the bridle through the maze of stumps into the woods on the opposite side.

"You oughta hold onto that black animal of yours," he called back over his shoulder.

"I will if I could only find him again. Have you seen him, Mr. Snape?"

"Look," the logging boss said, not unkindly, "I only work here, so don't ask questions I'm not supposed to answer."

"But you helped me once before, when we were here last February. You said we'd find Fury in that clearing and we did."

Snape turned and flashed his broken-toothed smile. "No kiddin'? Hey, that's great. See, kid, I'm not such a bad guy after all."

"No, you're not; you're okay. Now won't you please tell me if you've seen my horse?"

"Ask the boss. Anythin' like that's his business."

Snape faced forward again, and led the pony across the skid trail onto Yancey's property. The tract was an eyesore, a desolation of rotting stumps and dead branches. The logging boss had nothing more to say until he led the pony up a narrow path to a small shingled house surrounded by rude log cabins. A one-story shed lay behind the house.

"This here's the lumber camp," Snape said. "The house is where the boss lives."

A screen door opened and Yancey appeared on the top step. He wore a heavy work shirt and carried a rifle under his arm.

"Look who's here, boss," Snape called. "The kid from the ranch, the one that owns the black horse."

Yancey glowered at Joey. "Is he alone?"

"Yep. Rode up all by himself."

"How'd he come? Up the skid road?"

"Nope, right through the woods from the other side."

Yancey's face clouded. "How much did he see?"

"Enough to find out what's goin' on. This kid's pretty smart."

"Tie the horse to the railing here and get back to work. I'll talk to him alone."

Snape followed orders. "Take it easy," he whispered as Joey dismounted. "Don't say anythin' you don't hafta say. Just ask him about your black horse."

"What're you saying to him?" Yancey shouted.

"Nothin'. Told him to be careful gettin' down, that's all."

Yancey grunted. "Now get back to the job."

As Snape walked away, Yancey came down the steps and took Joey roughly by the arm. "This is the third time you've come nosin' around my place. What're you lookin' for this time?"

Joey felt weak in the knees. "My horse, Mr. Yancey. He broke out again last night."

"Is he after that white mare again?"

"Yes, sir, we think so."

"What makes you think he might be around here?"

"Well, he was here before and — well — I just have to look everywhere till I find him."

"You look on Blazin' Ridge?"

"Yes, sir, but he wasn't there. I didn't see any signs of the mustangs at all."

"But you saw some other kind of signs, didn't you?"

Joey swallowed a lump in his throat. "I — I don't know what you mean."

Yancey tightened his grasp on Joey's arm. "Now look, don't lie to me! What'd you see when you rode through the tall timber? Answer me!"

"I saw the government warnings."

"And what else?"

"I saw your lumberjacks cutting the trees that aren't supposed to be cut."

Yancey's eyes flashed. "So what now? What're you goin' to do about it?"

"I don't know — honest. I haven't had time to think. All I want is my stallion. Have you seen him?"

"What I've seen isn't important. The main thing is what you've seen."

Feeling a sudden hatred for the man, Joey forgot his fears and the words rushed out in a torrent, accusingly. "You're timber rustling, Mr. Yancey! You're cutting trees that belong to the United States government and that's a Federal crime!"

Yancey's face turned scarlet. "You don't know what you're talkin' about!"

"Yes I do! That's public-domain land, and when the foresters find out what you're doing, you'll be charged with timber trespass."

The angry lumberman dropped Joey's arm and stepped backward. "That's mighty big talk. If you rode up here alone, who's goin' to tell the foresters about it?"

Joey felt his fears returning. "I don't know. I — I just know that stealing trees from the government is a crime."

Yancey's voice was hard and rasping. "You've got to understand one thing, so listen to me. If you ever say a word about this — to anybody — I'm goin' to use *this!*" He brought his rifle up and prodded Joey in the ribs.

Joey felt the blood draining from his face, and spoke in a whisper. "You'd . . . *kill* me?"

Yancey tucked the weapon under his arm. "It's not you I'd shoot."

"What do you mean? I don't understand."

Yancey started walking around the side of the house. "Follow me and I'll show you."

He led Joey to the tool shed, a long low structure that housed logging equipment. There were no windows in the building and the door was fastened by a steel slide bar and a metal chain.

Yancey looked around. "What's your stallion's name again?"

"Fury. Why?"

"Call his name."

"What for?"

"Don't argue. Call his name."

Joey's lower jaw dropped. "Is Fury in here?" The man nodded. "I don't believe it."

"Call him."

Half-believing, Joey took a deep breath and called, "Fury!"

There was a sudden stirring inside the shed, followed by the sharp crack of hoofs against the door.

"Fury!" Joey cried.

The stallion answered with a sound that was half-whinny, half-whistle. The door trembled as he threw his weight against it.

Joey turned. "He is in there! You found him!"

"That's right, we did."

"How? When?"

"Last night, when he came chasin' through here with that wild mare. It took four of us to rope him and lock him up."

Joey caught hold of the slide bar, but before he could push it sideways, Yancey knocked his hand down.

"No you don't. We got a little talkin' to do before you let that horse out."

"About what?"

Yancey patted his rifle. "This."

Fury whistled again and his hoofs drummed on the door.

"I'll let you have a look at him," Yancey said. "Then we'll talk."

He slid the bolt, allowing the door to open about six inches. The chain kept it from opening any wider. Fury's muzzle appeared through the narrow opening, the nostrils dilating. Joey ran his hand across the soft, dark skin.

"Gosh, Fury, I've been riding all over the mountains trying to find you."

"You like him a lot, don't you, kid?"

"Yes, sir. Now I'm going to let him out." Joey's hand darted to the chain.

"Don't touch that chain!" Yancey raised his rifle and pointed it toward the opening. The barrel was aimed at a spot midway between Fury's wild eyes. The man's finger curled around the trigger.

"Don't!" Joey cried. *"Don't!"* Leaping forward, he attempted to push the rifle aside.

Without lowering the weapon, Yancey raised his right leg and kicked at Joey with his heavy boot. The chain rattled as Fury snorted and threw his body against the door.

"One more fool trick like that," Yancey warned, "and you'll have a dead horse."

"No! You can't kill him! You can't!"

Yancey brought the rifle down. "Sure I can — any time I feel like it. Right now, or some night when he's standin' in his corral down on the ranch. What happens to him is up to you."

Bewildered, Joey shook his head. "What do you mean? What do you want me to do?"

"It's not what I want you to do. It's what I want you *not* to do. You're supposed to be smart. You must know what I'm talkin' about."

Joey hesitated for a moment. "You mean about timber rustling?"

Yancey's eyes narrowed. "What timber rustlin'? You didn't see anythin' like that, now did you?"

"No, sir," Joey said in a strangled voice. "I didn't see anything like that."

"Sure, that's easy to say right now, when I've got this gun pointed at your horse's head. But what're you goin' to say later, when you're back at the ranch?"

"I don't know, Mr. Yancey. I — I hadn't thought."

The lumberman lowered the weapon and grabbed Joey's arm. "Okay then, I'll tell you what to think. You're goin' to think to yourself: If I ever tell a soul about what I saw, my horse is goin' to get killed." He slapped the stock of his rifle. "Is that clear?"

Joey's heart was pounding. "But what if somebody else finds out about your timber rust . . . I mean about what you're doing up here?"

"Nobody will; I'll see to that. So if any government men ever come around my loggin' operation, I'll know who sent 'em up here. And this horse of yours will be dead. Understand?"

Joey glanced at Fury. "Yes, sir."

"That's better. Now raise your right hand and take an oath you won't tell." Joey hesitated. "Do as I say! Swear it on Fury's life!"

Joey's right arm shot up. "I swear it on Fury's life."

"Okay. Now tell your horse to stand away from the door."

"Get back, Fury. Get back inside."

Fury withdrew his head from the opening. With the rifle tucked under his arm, Yancey released the chain and swung the door open. As Fury rushed from the shed and stood blinking in the sunlight, Joey ran to him and threw his arms around the muscular neck. Fury gave a snort of welcome, then whirled upon Yancey and raised himself on his hind legs. With a scream of fear, Yancey dropped the rifle and threw his arms up to shield his head from the raking hoofs.

"Get him out of here! Take him away!"

"Down, Fury, down!" Joey commanded. Grasping the flying mane, he vaulted to Fury's back and brought him under control.

Yancey retreated to the safety of the shed and called out through the door, "That horse is a killer! If I had my gun I'd shoot him right now!"

Joey slid from Fury's back, picked up the rifle, and remounted.

"I'll leave your gun at the end of the path!" he shouted. "And don't ever think again about killing Fury, because I swore I wouldn't tell — and I won't!"

At Yancey's house Joey untied the calico pony and led it by the bridle down the path. When he had ridden a safe distance he leaned down and placed the rifle upon a stump. Several hours later he came to the meadow and headed for the BW, burdened by the terrible secret which he had sworn on Fury's life never to reveal.

Chapter 5
AUNT MAGGIE

During the week that followed, the second week of August, Jim, Pete, and the hired hands rounded up a fresh stock of mustangs, and a heavy schedule of ranch work began. Joey did his share, although he seemed unusually quiet and thoughtful.

"That boy ain't sleepin' so good," Pete told Jim one morning. "Jest before sunup I went to the kitchen to git me a drink of water, and danged if he wasn't paddin' around the house in his pajammers."

"There's something on his mind," said Jim, "and it's probably Fury, as usual. I'm sure he lives in constant fear that Fury will run off again."

"If on'y that danged dog hadn't took a shine to Packy everythin'd be okay. As long as Crosby was here, Fury never give a thought to that white mare."

"Well, Crosby belongs to Packy now for certain, but I don't think Fury minds. When Packy rode over

64

here yesterday, Fury didn't give the dog more than a careless glance."

"I'm shore glad of that, Jim, 'cause I wouldn't want that horse to be jealous of Packy. If he was, the little tyke'd never be able to come over here agin."

The men stepped out to the porch.

"Fury seems pretty settled now," Jim said. "Let's hope he'll stay that way for a few weeks. If he doesn't, we'll have to ride up and bring the white mare down here."

Pete pushed his hat back with his thumb. "Joey won't like that a bit, an' that's a fact."

"We'll cross that bridge when we come to it. Meanwhile, let's get the day's work started. Rouse the hands and hop to it."

Day after day the BW lay under a cloud of dust, as the bronc twisters schooled the mustangs. Development of the green stock into first-class cow horses required careful handling, and Jim saw to it that they were not overworked. He knew from experience that slow, steady schooling always produced better results than fast work, and that a firm hand and a friendly manner kept a freshly broken bronc from becoming excited and turning into an unruly mount.

Each morning Packy rode over on Lucky, with Crosby romping beside them. As Jim had pointed out, Fury hardly noticed the dog's existence. During the afternoons and early evenings Joey spent hours trying to teach the younger boy to throw a rope.

"Why is it called a lariat?" Packy asked.

"It comes from a Spanish word," Joey explained. "*Reata*. It means 'rope.'"

"Then what's a lasso?"

"That comes from a Spanish word, too. *Lazo*, meaning a snare or a trap."

"Boy, you sure know a lot about it."

"I ought to. When I first came here, Jim gave me a book and I studied up on it. There are so many different names for catch ropes I can hardly remember them all."

"What're some of them?"

Joey ticked off the names on his fingers. "Well, let's see. There's throw rope, saddle rope, catch rope, twine, whale line, hard twist, and plenty more that I can't think of."

Packy sighed. "Gee, I'll be lucky if I just remember the word rope. Hey, give me that rope a second and let me see if I can lasso Crosby."

"You haven't got a chance. He's too lively and you're not half good enough yet."

"Then you try to catch him."

"Okay, watch this. It's an overhead swing."

Joey swung the loop over his head in a horizontal circle and threw it at the prancing dog. Crosby ducked as he saw the loop coming, then took the rope in his teeth and backed away, growling.

Packy shrieked with laughter. "You sure missed him that time. Try it once more."

"You try it," said Joey listlessly. "I'm tired."

Packy tried to get the rope away from Crosby, but gave up when the dog pulled him over on his face.

"When I learn to throw a rope like a real cowhand," Packy said, "I'm going up to Mr. Yancey's place and lasso him and tie him to a tree."

Joey glanced suddenly toward the distant hills. "Why'd you have to bring *him* up?" he asked huskily.

Packy scowled. "Hey Joey, what's wrong with you? Every time anybody mentions Mr. Yancey's name you get all white. What really happened when you went up there to find Fury? Did you have a fight or something?"

"Look, forget it, will you?"

"Okay," said Packy in a hurt tone.

Joey turned abruptly and ran down to Fury's corral. Packy stayed behind to play tug of war with Crosby.

"Are you all right, Fury?" Joey whispered.

The stallion whinnied gently and nuzzled the boy's shoulder.

"I can't tell anybody what really happened. I can't ever tell; I swore it on your life." Joey looked out toward Blazing Ridge, which stood red against the sky in the setting sun. "I even had to lie to Jim and Pete," he said bitterly, "and I've never done that before. When I brought you back that day, I told them I'd found you in the clearing behind Mr. Yancey's place. I didn't dare tell them the truth, or Mr. Yancey'd be arrested for cutting those government trees and — and then he'd have you killed somehow." He broke into a sob. "It's awful, Fury! I don't know what to do!"

Climbing the fence, he sat on the top rail stroking Fury's neck until Packy rode down to say so long.

On the morning of the fifteenth, Jim and Joey put on clean Levis and California shirts and climbed into the station wagon. Pete stood on the top step of the porch with a sour expression on his face.

"Sure you don't want to come along?" Jim called.

"I druther die," the old foreman answered sullenly.

"Aw, come on, Pete," Joey pleaded. "It'll be fun for the three of us to go."

"Dry up," said Pete. "I'd sooner be buried bare in an anthill."

Jim chuckled. "But what'll we tell her when you're not there to meet her?"

"Tell her I'm snakebit; say I been cow-kicked; or jest say I hung meself to a rafter. I don't give a owl's hoot what you say, but I'll be shot fer a jackrabbit if I leave you drag me to the railroad to meet yer Aunt Maggie!"

"Okay," said Jim, "have it your way. I'll tell her you stayed home baking a cake with 'WELCOME' on it."

"You do an' I'll shave yer gizzard with a hay rake!" The stubborn old foreman glared at Jim angrily, then turned and shuffled into the house.

The telegram announcing Aunt Maggie's arrival had been phoned to Jim the night before.

"We'd better get some soap and water and do a little house cleaning," he said, as he hung up.

Pete bristled. "Whattya mean? This place is so clean we could eat off the floor, without even gittin' dust on our whiskers."

"Maybe so, but I think Aunt Maggie's more accustomed to eating from a table."

Pete dropped an iron frying pan that narrowly missed his foot. "Great balls o' fire! I plumb fergot about that woman! Was it her that phoned?"

"That was her telegram. She's arriving tomorrow morning by train."

"Hey, that's great," Joey said. "I can hardly wait to meet her."

Pete looked horrified. "Have you went plumb loco? Once that bossy female takes over, this here ranch won't be fit to live on."

"Who said she was bossy?" Jim asked.

"I said it, that's who said it!"

"But you've never even met her," Joey said.

"I don't hafta meet her. I tole you once before, a horse ranch ain't no place fer a woman."

"Well, simmer down and break out the mop," Jim ordered. "She'll be here in the morning, and we want this house to shine."

Pete threw his hands up. "Wal, that cooks it. I oughta died when I was a baby."

The three pitched in together, and after a few hours most of the ranch house sparkled like a diamond.

"I got a crick in me back that'll never straighten out," Pete complained, as he wrung out the mop. "I ain't worked so hard since I cooked four meals a day fer forty-seven bronc busters. But it's all done now, an' I must say the ole place looks purty good."

"It isn't over yet," said Jim. "We've still got your bedroom to clean."

Pete's jaw dropped. "Whattya mean? That ole battle-axe ain't never goin' to set foot in my room. I'm goin' to lock the door an' hide the key."

"That's all right with me, but we're going to clean it anyway. Mix up some more suds and let's get cracking."

It was one o'clock in the morning when Pete finally put on his long white nightshirt and crawled into bed, still grumbling about the injustice of it all.

"This is the end," he muttered, staring at the ceiling. "Good-bye, happiness. So long, peace an' quiet."

He was trying hard to think of something else to say farewell to, when his mouth fell open and he began to snore.

In the railroad station, Jim and Joey learned that the train from the East was on time and due in twenty minutes. When it pulled in, they craned their necks to find Aunt Maggie among the descending passengers.

"I don't know what she looks like," Joey said, "so you'd better point her out to me."

"I will, if I recognize her myself. I haven't seen her for a long time. . . . Oh, there she is — I think."

Jim hurried up to a white-haired woman who was standing beside a pile of luggage. "Aunt Maggie?" he said, removing his hat.

The woman glared at him. "Aunt *Maggie?* Young man, don't be ridiculous!"

"Oh, my mistake. I'm sorry." Jim wiped his brow and backed away.

"Boy, I'm glad she isn't Aunt Maggie," Joey whispered. "Pete would've been right."

Jim turned quickly as he heard a pleasant voice calling his name. "No mistake this time, Joey. Come on."

Aunt Maggie smiled warmly and offered her cheek for Jim to kiss.

"It's just wonderful to see you, Jim. It's been ages."

"It certainly has, Aunt Maggie, and Joey and I are delighted to see you."

"So this is Joey. I'm so pleased to meet you, dear."

Joey blushed slightly as she kissed him. "Thank you, Miss Newton. I'm pleased to meet you, too."

"Won't you please call me Aunt Maggie?"

"Yes, ma'am, I'd like to."

"We've got the car parked on the other side," Jim said. "Give me a hand with these bags, will you, Joey?"

Aunt Maggie was tall and vigorous-looking, with a face that seemed sunny and cheerful beneath a crown of auburn braids that were threaded with gray. She was dressed neatly in a dark green suit, black stockings, sensible black shoes, and a small hat with a flower in it. Her strides, as she walked, were not quite as long as Jim's, and every now and then she gave a little spring in order to keep up with him.

As soon as Joey had stowed the bags in the station wagon, they began their drive back to the Broken Wheel.

"Such magnificent country," Aunt Maggie said, inhaling deeply. "And this glorious air — mm — it's just like wine."

Joey had never thought of air as being anything like wine, but he decided not to ask her to explain until he knew her a little better.

As they sped along, Jim and Joey pointed out the buttes, the mountains, and other interesting aspects of the terrain; and Aunt Maggie expressed genuine admiration for all of them. Finally, she changed the subject.

"You were both so kind to meet me at the station, but I really expected to see three of you. Where's the man you call Pete?"

Joey spoke up. "Oh, he didn't feel like com . . ."

Jim coughed and broke in quickly. "Pete stayed at the ranch to get the noon meal ready. He — uh — he was sorry that he wasn't able to come with us."

"I'm sorry, too, because I'm terribly eager to meet him. Your letters have made him seem like a very colorful person."

"He's that all right," Jim agreed. "And he's been excited ever since he heard you were coming."

Joey stifled a giggle with his hand, and Aunt Maggie turned around.

"What are you laughing at, dear?"

Joey straightened his face quickly. "Oh, I wasn't laughing," he fibbed. "I was sneezing." He faked a sneeze to prove it.

"Gracious, you must be catching a cold. You'd better run the window up. And as soon as we arrive at the ranch, I'll give you two cold tablets out of my medicine kit."

"Don't bother, Aunt Maggie. I'll be okay."

She reached back and gave him a motherly pat. "We must keep you healthy, Joey. As I always say: An ounce of prevention is worth a pound of cure."

"Yes, ma'am, I guess it is."

When she expressed her curiosity about Fury he warmed up to her, and spent the remainder of the journey describing how Jim and Pete had lured the great, wild stallion to the ranch, and how he himself had been the first and only human to ride and tame him.

As they drove through the gate, Fury pranced about, making loud noises of welcome.

"There's Fury," Joey said proudly. "Isn't he great?"

"He certainly is. I've never seen such a magnificent stallion."

"Well, here we are," said Jim, as they pulled up at the house. "This is our valley home."

"It's beautiful," Aunt Maggie said. "I just know I'm going to love it."

"We have the spare room all ready for you. Joey, help me take the bags in, and as soon as Aunt Maggie has made herself comfortable, we'll have dinner."

Aunt Maggie seemed surprised to hear that they were having dinner at midday. "I really couldn't eat a great deal," she said apologetically, "so perhaps I'll just have a fruit salad and a cup of tea."

"Hm," said Jim thoughtfully. "I don't think Pete's ever made a fruit salad, but I'm sure you can show him how." As his aunt was walking up the porch steps he whispered to Joey. "Look on the shelf in the food locker and see if you can find a can of fruit."

"Pete'll hit the ceiling," Joey whispered back. "He's cooking corned beef and cabbage and home-fried potatoes."

Aunt Maggie called from the porch. "I'm terribly anxious to meet Pete. Where is he, Jim?"

"Probably in the kitchen. First let us show you to your room."

After the visitor had closed her door, they went looking for Pete. The dinner was cooking on the stove, but the old man had vanished.

73

"Go find him," Jim said. "Hurry. I'll watch the food."

Joey scurried out through the kitchen door, and returned in a few minutes with a look of concern on his face.

Jim looked up from the stove. "Did you find him?"

"I sure did."

"Where?"

"He's hiding in the hayloft. He won't come down."

"He won't come. . . ? That's ridiculous." Jim wiped his hands on a towel. "Look for that can of fruit. I'll be right back."

In the hayloft Pete was lying on a bale of straw, with his arms folded under his head. Jim pulled him roughly to his feet.

"Leggo of me!" Pete yowled.

Jim held on. "Are you out of your mind? Come on. Aunt Maggie's here."

"Yer tellin' me! I snuck a look out the kitchen winder when she got outa the car. She looks even worse'n I thought."

"Nonsense. She's a very nice woman. Now come along and quit sulking."

The old man stuck his lower lip out. "I ain't sulkin'. I'm jest standin' on my rights as a male human bein'."

"Well, come back anyway. You've got to fix my aunt a fruit salad."

Pete looked as though he had been struck between the eyes. "A fruit *salad*? What're we runnin' here, a horse ranch or a tearoom?" He curled his lip. "Before I'd fix a fruit salad I'd sooner be nibbled by ducks!"

"Okay, I'll fix it. But you've got to come and meet Aunt Maggie, and treat her like a gentleman. I mean it, Pete. She's our guest, and as long as she's here we're going to make her feel welcome."

Pete's eyes wavered. "Wal, okay, I'll do the best I kin, dang it. But see that the ole biddy stays outa my hair."

Jim ruffled the three strands of hair that were strung there for her to stay out of.

When they returned to the kitchen, Joey had found a can of fruit. While Pete grumbled over the stove, Jim arranged the fruit neatly on leaves of fresh lettuce, then made a pot of tea. Before the meal was quite ready, Aunt Maggie came into the kitchen. She had changed into a gray linen dress.

"Well now," Jim said enthusiastically, "you certainly look lovely."

She tilted her head. "Why thank you, Jim. That's a sweet compliment."

Pete hastily jammed his shirttail into his jeans and turned. On his face was a mirthless smile that did full justice to his store teeth.

"Now, Aunt Maggie," Jim said, "I'd like you to meet the real boss of the BW — my foreman, Pete Wilkie."

She extended her hand graciously. "I'm delighted to meet you, Pete."

"Likewise," Pete said, wiping his palm on his shirt and shaking her hand limply.

Aunt Maggie glanced at the table. "How nice. You've prepared my salad and tea."

He lowered his eyes. "I didn't do it; Jim did."

"Joey," said Jim, "while we're putting the dinner on, why not show my aunt the rest of the house?"

"I'd like to. Come on, Aunt Maggie, we've got lots of wonderful things in the living room. Guns, powder horns, Indian arrowheads, and stuff like that."

Jim watched them go, then clapped Pete on the back. "Thanks a lot for acting like a gentleman. How do you like her?"

"She ain't bad — so far. But she jest got here. Wait'll she digs her claws in an' starts gittin' bossy."

"Well, grin and bear it. She'll only be with us for a few weeks."

"That's what *you* think." Pete scowled. "This's the first time in my life I've ever wisht fer a busted leg. Then I'd be took to a nice, quiet hospital till the storm blows over."

"You'll change your tune when you see what a fine person she is."

"Shore, shore, she's a reg'lar queen. But I'll tell you, Jim, our bach'lor days is over. C'mon, let's rustle this grub onto the table."

Pete said little during the meal, except when asked direct questions by their guest, at which times his answers were polite but short. Joey and Jim, on the other hand, enjoyed telling her all about the daily routine of a busy horse ranch. At the end of the meal Pete jumped to his feet.

"C'mon, Joey. Let's manicure the golden dishes."

"Let's what?" asked Aunt Maggie, perplexed.

Joey grinned. "He means clean up."

"Really? What a colorful expression."

"Pete uses quite a few colorful expressions," Jim said, after the other two had left. "Words and phrases he picked up during his many years as a cowhand."

"But won't they have a poor influence upon Joey's English?"

"I don't think so. Joey doesn't use them himself."

Jim spent the next hour taking his aunt on a walking tour of the corrals and stables. She seemed greatly impressed by the efficiency of the establishment, and proved to Jim that she knew a great deal about horses. Joey caught up with them as they were strolling by the barn.

"Goodness, Joey," said Aunt Maggie, "that reminds me. I must give you those pills for your cold. I'll get them as soon as we return to the house."

Joey cast a guilty glance at Jim. "Thanks, but my cold's all gone now. I guess I just had a little sniffle."

"You seem so far away from things way out here. Jim, is there a good, reliable doctor you can call upon in case of sickness?"

"There's one in town, but we hardly ever have any need for him. Unless there's a serious illness, we doctor ourselves."

"But good health is so terribly important, especially in a growing boy." She turned to Joey. "You seem a trifle underweight for your height, Joey dear. I have an excellent blood tonic in my kit. I'll give you a spoonful this evening."

Joey winced. "I don't feel underweight. I really feel kind of heavy."

"He's a remarkably healthy boy," said Jim. "Working with horses keeps him fit."

"I'm sure of that, Jim. But 'a sound mind in a sound body' has always been my motto."

As the days passed, and Aunt Maggie settled into the routine of the ranch, she began making small changes, a few at a time. Her first project was to make curtains for the windows. Her reasons for doing so, she explained logically, were "hominess and privacy."

"Privacy, my hind leg!" Pete growled, the first time he saw the colored gingham at the living room windows. "We're miles from our nearest neighbor. Who's goin' to peek in at us?"

"Simmer down," Jim told him. "You must admit the house does look better than it did with bare windows."

"Wal, she ain't goin' to hang no lace drawers on *my* winder! My bedroom door's locked, an' the key's stuck in my boot."

Jim chuckled. "I wondered why you've been limping for the past week."

Aunt Maggie's next projects were to make the men wear neckties at the table; to put them on a diet containing fewer fats and more vitamins; to carry the dishes out a few at a time, instead of piling them into a stack; and to go to bed earlier.

When Joey protested this final direction, she argued him down with a quotation from Ben Franklin: "Early to bed and early to rise, makes a man healthy, wealthy, and wise."

"Bushwa!" Pete mumbled later. "She oughta take a look at our mailman. He's in bed at eight an' up at four; an' he's sickly, poor, an' stupid!"

Aunt Maggie's intentions were kind, but it was difficult for the Broken Wheelers to change their living habits so suddenly. Even Jim experienced some discomfort under the new regime, but was too fond of his aunt to suggest that she ease the pressure.

"She'll be leaving soon," he told the others at the end of August, "so let's not argue with her. As soon as she goes, everything will run smoothly again."

"But when's she goin'?" Pete insisted. "Give us the exact date."

"I don't know the exact date. She and I haven't discussed it. But she said she'd stay just a few weeks, and it's been two already. So try to be patient for just a little longer."

"Gosh," Joey said, "it's kind of hard to be patient. I really like her, Jim, honest; but I wish she'd quit talking about germs all the time, and making me take medicine from that darn kit of hers."

Jim smiled. "You brought that on yourself that time in the station wagon when you faked a sneeze."

Two more weeks went by, during which Aunt Maggie made no mention of going home. By degrees, she had completely taken over the management of the house. Although Pete was secretly relieved that he no longer had to cook or clean, he passed the days in sullen silence.

One day in mid-September his dislike for Aunt Maggie reached its climax. Returning to the house he found that she had picked the lock of his bedroom door with a hairpin and hung blue calico curtains at his window.

"That cooks it!" he yelled, as he stomped out and slammed the door. "Till that den mother leaves the BW, I'm sleepin' in the bunkhouse!"

Chapter 6
ANGEL

"**D**oggone it," said Packy gloomily, "here it is the end of September and I still haven't learned how to throw a rope. I can't even settle a loop on a fence post."

"It'll be a lot easier when you get taller," Joey assured him. "I wasn't so good myself at first." He eyed Packy's lunch box, hungrily. "Hey, are you going to eat all that chocolate cake?"

"Why? You want a hunk?"

"I sure do. When Aunt Maggie packs my school lunch, she never puts in dessert. She says too much sweet stuff is bad for my skin."

"Aw, that's a lot of baloney. Here, grab some cake. I was going to give it to Crosby, but I guess you need it more than he does."

"Thanks, you're a real pal."

The dog sat next to Joey, raising and lowering his head each time Joey lifted his arm to bite off a piece of the cake. When he realized he wasn't going to get even a crumb, he ambled off to see what the other children in the schoolyard might have to offer.

"How soon is Jim's aunt going back home?" Packy asked.

"Gee, I don't know. Neither does Jim."

"Why doesn't he ask her?"

"He can't. It wouldn't be polite."

"Why not?"

"Well gosh, Packy, she's his father's sister. He can't say to her, 'Look, you've been here six weeks now, when're you leaving?' "

"Well, *I'd* sure ask her. A female on a ranch can cause a lot of trouble."

Joey laughed. "You've been listening to Pete."

Packy peeled an orange. "Boy, old Pete sure has changed. He hardly even says hello to me and Crosby anymore. Is he still sleeping in the bunkhouse?"

"No, Jim made him move back to his room. He told him to quit acting like a spoiled brat."

"What'd Pete say to that?"

"He got mad, but he finally came back. And you know the first thing he did when he got to his room? He yanked down Aunt Maggie's blue curtains and hung up a piece of burlap instead."

Packy giggled. "Boy, that's funny. Did she get mad when she saw it?"

"Nope, she never gets mad. She just smiled and said, 'Your new curtain looks lovely, Pete. You have excellent taste.' That made him madder than ever."

"You know something? I think Aunt Maggie's kind of nice."

"So do I. I really like her, when she's not after me to take medicine." Joey spoke wistfully. "It's kind of nice to have her around. It's almost like — well — having a mother."

When school was over for the day, the boys rode back to the BW together. When Crosby spied Aunt Maggie sweeping the porch, he ran to her and nipped at her broom. She patted his head for a minute, then suddenly picked him up in her arms.

"Watch your clean dress," Joey warned. "He's real dirty."

"I know. That's why I picked him up. Get a bar of yellow soap and bring it out to the horse trough."

"Okay."

Packy was shocked. "You're not going to give him a bath, are you?"

"I certainly am. I've been trying to catch this dog and give him a good scrubbing ever since I first met him."

"He'll hate it. He's never had a bath in his whole life."

"Well, he's going to get one now. Come on, Packy, you can help."

When Crosby was dunked into the trough, he squirmed like an eel and set up a howl that could be heard halfway across the valley. When the bath was over, he looked like an entirely different dog.

"Gosh," Joey said. "I never realized his gray spots were really white spots."

"Neither did I," Packy said disgustedly. "I liked him much better when he was dirty."

The moment Aunt Maggie released Crosby, he ran down to Fury's corral and rolled in the dust. When he was satisfied that he was good and dirty again, he nipped at Fury's legs, inviting him to play. The horse turned his back to Crosby and lashed out at him with his hind hoofs. Whimpering with surprise and fright, the dog wormed hastily through the bars and ran to Packy for protection.

Aunt Maggie, who had been watching, shook her head.

"What's the matter?" Joey asked.

"I'm worried about that stallion of yours, Joey. There's still a streak of wildness in him that might be dangerous."

"He's not wild," Joey said indignantly. "He's as tame as can be."

"I'm not so sure about that. And I'm much too fond of you to see you get hurt. I think I'd better have a talk with Jim."

"Wait!" Joey called, as she strode toward the barn. "Fury wouldn't ever hurt me. I'm his friend."

Aunt Maggie found Jim in the loft, checking the feed supply.

"Welcome," he said, surprised. "You came up that ladder like an athlete."

She smiled. "Oh, there's plenty of life left in the old girl yet. Jim, may I talk to you for a moment?"

"Why certainly." He frowned. "Anything serious?"

"Well, it could be. Actually it's about Fury. I've been watching him carefully, and he seems to be getting more excitable every day."

"I've noticed that, too. I'm sure he has the white mare on his mind."

"If that's the cause of his skittishness, he could actually become dangerous. I was brought up with horses, Jim, so you can be sure I know what I'm talking about. If Joey continues to ride him, he might be badly injured — even killed."

Jim looked grave. "What're you suggesting, Aunt Maggie?"

"That Fury be sold or turned loose in the hills."

Jim walked silently to the door of the loft and looked down at the corral. Fury was racing around the enclosure and Joey was seated on the fence, imploring him to calm down. Jim drew a deep breath and returned to his aunt.

"I'm sorry, but I can't accept either of your suggestions. That horse is Joey's whole life."

Aunt Maggie spoke quietly. "If Joey had a mother — how would she feel about it? Would she want his life to be endangered?"

"I don't know," Jim answered sharply. "He has no mother, but he does have a father. At least he's accepted me as a father ever since I adopted him from the Home. And, as a father, I can tell you bluntly that I will not separate my son from his horse. Fury's staying on the ranch."

"Very well, Jim. If that's your decision, so be it. And now I'd like to ask you something else, and I'd appreciate your speaking frankly."

"I always do, Aunt Maggie. What is it?"

"I'd like to know whether I'm welcome or unwelcome on this ranch."

Jim was taken aback by the abruptness of the question. "You're welcome, of course. When you first suggested this visit I wrote that you could come and stay as long as you liked."

"That's true, and I'm grateful for your hospitality." She moved to the door and looked out over the broad valley. "I've learned to love this part of the West, Jim. And I love you and Joey — and yes — even Pete. I've lived most of my years alone, and I've never known the joys of family life until I came to the Broken Wheel. I know I've caused dissension here from time to time, but I also believe that I've not been wholly useless. Most importantly, I think that Joey has come to accept me as a — I was going to say mother — but I'll say friend."

"He has, Aunt Maggie. He likes you very much. And you have been useful to us in many ways," he smiled ruefully, "despite some grumbling in certain quarters."

"Yes, Pete — dear old Pete — I think he rather enjoys being miserable. But it isn't Pete that matters to me, it's Joey." She looked up into Jim's face. "And now, for Joey's sake, I'm going to ask another bold question that calls for a frank answer."

"You'll get it."

"All right. Jim, may I stay a little longer at the Broken Wheel?"

He hesitated for a fraction of a second. "Of course you may, Aunt Maggie."

"Thank you, dear, thank you very much."

"However," Jim added, "there are two conditions. First, you must never speak again of our getting rid of Fury."

"Very well. And the second?"

He grinned. "And for the sake of peace and harmony, try to stay out of Pete's hair."

"Agreed," said Aunt Maggie.

Alone once again in the loft, Jim paced back and

forth trying to decide how he was going to break the news to the others. He broke it that evening behind the house, while his aunt was in the kitchen doing the dishes. To his satisfaction, Joey appeared somewhat pleased; and to his surprise, Pete didn't hit the ceiling.

"Shucks," the old man said, "I knowed it all along. When she didn't leave by the end of August, I knowed dang well she had it in her noodle to take root forever."

"It won't be forever," Jim argued. "As soon as winter threatens, I'm pretty sure she'll want to get back to Philadelphia."

"Phooey," said Pete. "She'll still be here when I'm stone, cold dead in the bone yard."

"What'd she say about Fury?" Joey asked. "She had some idea about my getting hurt or something."

"Don't worry about Fury. He's our business, not hers."

"Well then, everything's okay," Joey said cheerfully. He poked Pete in the ribs. "I guess it won't be so bad having a den mother after all."

As usual, since Aunt Maggie had pointed out the value of going to bed early and rising early, everyone was sleeping soundly by eleven o'clock. Fury, too, exhausted from his constant pacing during the day, lay quietly in the western corner of his corral. When the moon was directly overhead, he stirred in his sleep and awakened, quivering. Rising to his feet, he stood motionless for a moment, gazing upward toward the round disk of light. Responding to some sound, scent, or instinct, he brought his head down suddenly and faced westward. From the depths of his throat came a shrill, despairing cry — a sound that was a mixture of misery and excitement. Then, feeling a strong urge to be on the move, he galloped at high speed around the perimeter of his enclosure.

Joey was the first of the sleepers to hear the stallion's cry. Leaping from his bed, he ran into the living room calling frantically for Jim, who came quickly and turned on the light.

"I heard him," Jim said. "Jump into your clothes! We'll try to lock him in the barn before he breaks out!"

"Okay, but let's hurry!"

As they raced back into their rooms, Aunt Maggie emerged in a red housecoat, her hair done up in curlers. At the same moment Pete burst from his own bedroom, the tails of his long nightshirt flying.

"What is it?" he cried sleepily. "What's goin' on?"

"Jim! What happened?" Aunt Maggie asked fearfully, as Jim and Joey returned, zipping up their jackets.

"Fury's acting up. Where's Pete?"

"He was just here, but ran back for some reason."

"Come on, Pete!" Jim yelled. "Hurry it up!"

"I'm tryin' to git me pants on, dang it!" Pete replied from behind his closed door.

Joey was halfway down the road as Jim caught up to him. "Talk to him and keep talking!" Jim shouted. "I'll try to rope him as he runs by!"

Joey squirreled through the fence and held up his arms. "All right, Fury, take it easy! Easy, boy, easy! Come on now, calm down!"

Fury thundered toward Joey with his head down.

"On the fence!" Jim cried. "Climb up, Joey!"

Fury swerved as he came to Joey, and began another circle.

"I said on the fence! He's too spooked to know what he's doing!"

Straddling the top rail, Joey called Fury at the top of his voice. Jim had snatched a rope from the post and was standing on the hardpan, building a loop. As the screaming stallion came around again, Jim let the loop fly and picked up Fury's neck in a hoolihan catch. Jim dug his heels in, and the gravel sprayed up like snow before a plow. Fury was slowing down, as Pete and Joey rushed up and got hold of the rope. Joey went up the line, hand over hand, talking a blue streak to the thrashing horse.

It took twenty minutes to get the heaving stallion into the barn, and another hour to get him cooled and settled. By the time they had padlocked the door and returned to the house, the clock over the fireplace read two-thirty. In the kitchen Aunt Maggie had prepared a supper for the weary workers.

"I knew you'd want to talk before going back to bed, so sit right down and help yourselves."

"That's mighty thoughtful of you, Aunt Maggie," Pete said.

She beamed at the old man. It was the first time he had ever called her by that name. Heretofore it had been "Miss Newton" or "ma'am."

"I'd like to compliment all three of you," she said. "I was watching from the porch, and you handled that horse beautifully."

Jim held out his coffee cup for a refill. "Thanks,

but we couldn't have managed it without Joey. He displayed plenty of courage and know-how."

"I guess I did it without thinking," said Joey modestly. "I knew we had to catch him before he took off."

"You look plumb tuckered," said Pete. "Yer goin' to have a hard time keepin' yer eyes open in school tomorrow."

Joey glanced at Jim. "I guess I'll have to ride another horse to school. Fury'll need a good day's rest."

Jim drained his cup and sat back from the table. "Let's talk a few minutes about Fury."

"We better," Pete said. "This bus'ness of bein' routed outa bed in the middle of the night's givin' me the double-dyed jimjams."

"There's only one solution," Jim went on, "and I'm sure we all know what it is."

Joey looked up solemnly. "You mean the white mare?"

"Right. We've got to find her and bring her in."

"Tomorrow?"

"Yes, even though it means postponing other important work. I was going to finish the feed inventory, but I guess that job will have to wait."

Aunt Maggie broke in. "Why not let me do it, Jim?"

"You mean it?"

"Of course. I'm sure I could do it very well."

"I'm sure you could, too. Thanks for the offer; it's a deal."

Jim got the map from his desk and spread it out on the table.

"Pete and I'll have to start early in the morning, so before we go back to bed, we'd be smart to map out a route to follow."

They pored over the map, checking the water holes generally used by the mustang herds.

"We'll start at the buttes and work upward in a zigzag course," Jim decided finally. "That way it shouldn't be too hard to find the mare."

Joey looked at the route which Jim had marked with a red pencil. "You'll stick to this trail, won't you?" he asked anxiously. "You won't have to go near Mr. Yancey's place?"

"I hardly think so."

"No need to," Pete added. "If Yancey's still loggin' up there, the mustangs'll be keepin' their distance. Them power saws an' engines make too much noise."

Joey sighed with relief.

"You look dead on your feet," Jim said. "You'd better turn in."

"Okay, Jim. Thanks for helping with Fury. I'm sorry he caused you so much trouble."

"Forget it, son. It's all part of running a ranch."

Joey turned at the door. "Thanks, Aunt Maggie, for making supper for us. And thanks for helping Jim with the feed inventory. When I get home from school, I'll give you a hand."

"That's kind of you, dear, but I'm sure I'll be finished by that time." She kissed him. "Good night, Joey. Rest well."

Joey went to his room, his eyes already half-closed.

"Now you two men had better get to bed," said

Aunt Maggie. "And don't worry about being away from the ranch tomorrow. If anything important comes up, I'll take care of it."

"I'll bet you will at that," said Jim with a grin.

Shortly after sunup the men were in their saddles. Very few words were exchanged, as they rode to the edge of the meadow and turned south toward the buttes. Cutting westward, Jim took the lead up the slope and followed the edge of a box canyon. It was shaped like a horseshoe and its red walls dropped away in a sheer descent from the rim. Peering downward through the underbrush and scrub oaks, they saw nothing on the canyon floor but shale and fallen rocks.

"Wal," Pete muttered, "we struck out on our first try. There ain't no wild ones at the bottom of this canyon."

Jim studied the map. "Here's where we cut northwest. It's a quarter of a mile to the first water hole."

The sun warmed their backs as they rode into the clearing, where the water lay muddy and still. Jim pointed to the grass, which was straightening up after having been trampled by many unshod hoofs.

"The herd's just pulled out. A good-sized one, too, by the looks of it."

"Twen'y or thirty I reckon."

"At least. Take it easy from here on. We don't want to spook them, or we might be riding all day."

For an hour they followed a trail of fresh manure, which led downward. As the trees grew fewer and the trail widened, Pete drew even with Jim.

"Mebbe we're goin' to git a break," he said quietly. "Looks to me like the critters went down to the flatland."

"Let's hope so."

When they reached ground level, they saw a cloud of brown dust just settling to the south.

"We got our break all right," Jim said. "The main thing is to keep them from turning back up the slope into the timber."

"I hope they ain't spotted us. We'd hafta chase 'em to kingdom come an' back."

Jim pointed. "The dust is pretty thick around that mesa. I think the herd must've stopped on the other side."

As they approached the towering mesa, they heard a distant booming sound.

"They ain't jest hangin' around," Pete shouted. "Sounds like they're movin' pretty fast."

The two men brought their knees together, urging their mounts into a gallop. When they were fifty yards from the mesa, they saw swift movement at its base and pulled up sharply.

"Look alive!" Jim shouted. "They've turned!"

Pete gaped. "Jehoshaphat! They're comin' right at us!"

The dust cloud was boiling toward them, and the wild horses could be seen coming out of the dust, with a brown stallion in the lead. If Jim and Pete hadn't wheeled sharply, the speeding lead horse would have run them down. As he thundered by, they saw his red, flaring nostrils and his wild eyes. Behind his streaming tail came the mares, making a great sighing sound as they fought for breath. As they appeared in silhouette against the buttes, Jim flung his arm out.

"There she is! Look!"

Among her varicolored companions, the white mare gleamed like snow in the sunlight. Before the last of them had passed, Jim and Pete rode into the thick of them, their right hands reaching for their lariats.

"Ride her on the left side!" Jim cried. "I'll take the right!"

Terrified by the pursuing men, the white mare swiveled her head, stumbled, and broke stride. The riders came up swiftly, swinging their loops.

"Now, Pete, now!"

Both loops shot out together and settled upon the snowy neck. As the mare struggled to free herself, the men slowed down, keeping their ropes taut. By the time she surrendered, wailing with terror, the herd was out of sight.

"We've got a surprise for Joey," Jim said, as he looked her over. "This mare's in foal."

"Yer right," said Pete.

When the men brought the mare through the gate, Joey had just returned from school.

"Here they are, Aunt Maggie!" he called "They've got her!"

"The white mare?"

"Sure. Come on!"

"She'll need to be quiet for the rest of the day," Jim warned, as he led the mare into the barn. "Don't forget, she's not used to people."

"But let me come in for just a minute," Joey

begged. "I want to see what Fury does when he sees her."

"Okay, but neither of us is going to stay."

As Jim led the mare past Fury's stall, he looked at her silently, then leaned out to sniff her sides. When she had been backed into the adjoining stall, he sniffed her once again and made small, loving sounds. Still frightened, she sidled to the far side of her stall.

"Is she scared of him?" Joey asked, almost hopefully.

"Just for the moment. She'll settle down in a hurry after we've gone and she's had a chance to recognize him. Now come on, Joey. We'll all come back to see her after supper."

Supper, under Aunt Maggie's supervision, really turned out to be dinner. She had prepared an enormous rib roast with potatoes and onions, and added a cocoanut custard pie for good measure.

When the meal was over, Pete pushed his chair back and patted his stomach. "That wasn't a bad supper."

"Thank you," said Aunt Maggie.

"If you was to ask me, though, that pie coulda used jest one more egg."

"Go on," said Jim. "That's the best custard pie you ever ate, and you know it."

Pete disregarded the comment. "A mite more coc'nut wouldn'ta hurt, neither."

"I think you're right, Pete," Aunt Maggie agreed. "I'll remember that next time."

"Come on," Joey said impatiently. "Let's all go out and see the mare."

"Okay," said Jim. "She ought to be settled down by now."

They trooped out to the barn and stood in a group, admiring the timid newcomer. After greeting them, Fury stretched his neck over the barrier and nuzzled the mare fondly. She responded by lifting her head and nipping him gently on the left ear. He stomped his forefeet and whinnied with pleasure.

"Listen to him," Pete said. "He's the happiest horse in fourteen counties."

"I don't blame him," said Aunt Maggie. "She's lovely, just lovely."

Jim looked the mare over and nodded with satisfaction. "She's a beauty all right. One of the finest mares we've ever had at the BW. What do you think of her, Joey?"

"She's okay. When do you think she's going to have her foal?"

Jim studied the mare thoughtfully. "Well . . ."

"In late December," said Aunt Maggie, "or early January."

"I think you're right," said Jim.

Pete looked at her in surprise. "How do you know about such things?"

"I was raised with horses, Pete, down in the blue-grass country. I was assisting mares with their foals when I was twelve years old."

"Is that a fact?" said Pete. "I'll be jiggered."

Jim turned to Joey. "She's yours now, yours and Fury's. So I think you should have the honor of naming her."

Joey scratched his head. "Gosh, I don't know what to call her. Uh, how about Snow White?"

"That's turrible," Pete said. "Sounds like a movie or somethin'."

Joey thought a moment longer. "Snowball?"

"Not bad," Jim said. "What do you think, Aunt Maggie? Is Snowball a good name?"

"Well, not really. It would be all right for a frisky colt, I think, but not for this angelic creature."

"Hey!" Joey exclaimed. "I've got it!"

"What is it?" they all asked together.

"Angel."

And Angel it was.

Chapter 7
STALLION FIGHT

When it turned cold early in October, the valley dwellers agreed that an unusually severe winter was ahead, and began making preparations. Those who raised beef cattle rounded them up for shipment to market. Bulls were gathered close to feeding stations. Calves that were dropped late in the spring were branded and weaned, so that their mothers would have only themselves to look out for when the snow fell.

At the Broken Wheel Ranch, Jim, Pete, and several hired hands spent the first two weeks of the month repairing storm windows, storing feed, and building snow fences.

Since Angel's arrival, Fury had become as placid as a horse born in captivity. Day after day they frolicked together in the corral, or stood side by side soaking up the October sunshine. During school hours, when Fury was absent, Angel waited patiently at the far corner of the enclosure, her soft eyes watching the gate for his return. When Joey rode in and turned Fury loose in the corral, she loped gracefully to the opening in the fence and greeted her mate with loving sounds.

Although Joey realized that Fury had become an even more satisfactory horse because of Angel, he deeply resented the affection his horse displayed for her. Before Angel had come to the BW, Fury had paid slight attention to anyone but Joey. Now, however, except when he was riding, Joey found that he no longer had Fury wholly to himself. And even though the stallion seemed to like his master no less than before, Joey felt it just wasn't the same at all. He tried desperately to stifle his resentment of the white mare, but as the days passed, the feeling against her grew even stronger. I'm jealous of Angel, he told himself bitterly, plain jealous, just as I was when Fury first ran off and went to her.

One night, Joey rose from his bed, dressed quickly, and crawled quietly out the window. Tiptoeing down the gravel road, he entered the corral, slipped a rope around Angel's neck, and led her from the enclosure. Although seemingly puzzled by Joey's action, Fury made no sound, but trotted curiously along the fence as Joey led Angel toward the ranch gate, walking her on the grass so as not to awaken anyone in the house.

Far out on the meadow, Joey lifted the noose from Angel's neck and gave her a sharp slap on the rump.

"Go on!" he shouted. "Run! Get back to the herd!"

Startled but unhurt by the slap, Angel darted forward. Joey watched her until she was only a speck of white in the gloom, then turned and went back to the corral. Fury was waiting, his ears thrown forward.

"It's okay," Joey whispered as he climbed the fence. "Everything's going to be all right from now on."

With his arms around the stallion's neck, he sat on the top rail, talking to him softly until the sky in the east turned pink.

A few hours later, Pete knocked on Jim's door and went in.

Jim was lathering his face. "Good morning, Pete, what can I do for you?"

"I dunno, Jim, mebbe nothin'. But tell me, did you go out an' put Angel in the barn durin' the night?"

"No, why? Isn't she in the corral?"

"Nope. Fury's out there all by hisself, an' lookin' mighty forlorn."

Jim set his razor down. "Have you spoken to Joey?"

"I peeked in, but he was sound asleep."

"Well, go down and see if she's in the barn."

"Okay."

Jim had his clothes on when Pete returned.

"She ain't there, Jim. In fact, she ain't nowheres. I looked high an' low."

Jim slapped his fist into his palm. "So it's finally happened. I've been aware of Joey's resentment of

Angel for the past few days, but I didn't think he'd be foolish enough to do a thing like this."

"You think he turned her loose?"

"Of course. Make yourself scarce, Pete. I want to handle Joey alone. This is a father-and-son problem."

"You won't be too hard on him, will you, Jim?" Pete asked anxiously. "He ain't never made a kid mistake like this before."

"That's right, but this one sure is a whopper."

Jim went into Joey's room and closed the door. Scanning the room, he saw the rumpled clothing on the floor and the telltale marks of shoes on the windowsill. Pulling a chair up to the bed, he sat down and shook the sleeping boy by the shoulder. Joey opened his eyes and blinked.

"Jim! What's the matter?"

"Sit up," Jim said sternly. "I want to talk to you."

Joey sat up and shot a quick glance out the window toward the corral.

"You know Angel isn't there, don't you?" said Jim.

"Okay," said Joey defiantly, "I did it. I let her out."

"That's obvious. The question is: Why?"

"Because Fury's *my* horse, not hers!"

"But Angel belongs to the Broken Wheel Ranch! What right did you have to dispose of my property? Don't you realize that's almost as serious as stealing?"

Joey flinched under Jim's angry gaze. "It isn't stealing; you have plenty of horses."

"We have plenty of food, too, and plenty of clothing," Jim said. "Would you throw those things away if you didn't like their taste or their color?"

"It isn't the same thing. Angel made me feel sick! I hate her!"

"You're talking like a baby. Angel isn't a person; she's an animal, and a valuable one."

"Fury's even more valuable," Joey argued, "but she ruined him."

"Nonsense. She improved his disposition and made him more manageable than ever." Joey made a move to rise. "Stay where you are!" Jim commanded. "You're going to listen to me if I have to hog-tie you to the bedpost!"

Joey sat up straight in bed and folded his arms. "If you're so mad at me," he said insolently, "why don't you wallop me?"

"I will, if you don't change your tone. I've never used physical punishment on you, but there's a first time for everything. If you don't stop acting like a spoiled brat, I'll turn you over my knee and show you what it's like to be spanked."

Joey flushed. "I'm not a spoiled brat."

"Only a brat would've done what you did last night."

"I had to do it, Jim. And if Fury'd been your horse, you'd have done it yourself."

Jim shook his head. "That's the silliest statement you've ever made. If Fury *had* been my horse, I would've brought the mare down here last February."

"Then why didn't you do it anyway?"

"Because you were jealous of her, and I felt sorry for you."

"Who says I'm jealous?"

"I say it. And you know it."

Joey looked away. "I can't help feeling that way, Jim. Fury used to be my best friend, but now he doesn't give a darn for me."

"That's bushwa, as Pete would say. Fury's always ready and willing to take you anywhere you want to ride. Don't you think his loyalty should be respected, not treated with contempt?"

"What do you mean? I do respect his loyalty."

"By driving his mate away? That's a mighty poor way to show respect."

Joey turned his head away. "He can get along without her."

"Now you're talking like a child again. He can't get along without Angel, and you know it. His instinct is to have that mare beside him in his corral. When she isn't there, some strong force urges him to run away and look for her. And remember this, Joey, if Fury should run to the hills again, he might be lost to you forever."

"No! Don't say that! He'll always come back!"

"I doubt that. But if he does, we'll always have to keep him locked up in the barn."

"We can't lock him in the barn! Not Fury! It'd be like being in jail!"

"Exactly. Without his freedom his spirit would be broken, and he'd be second-rate." Jim pointed out the window. "Look at him. He's strong, active, and full of life. Do you want a spirited stallion, Joey, or would you prefer a meek, fat saddle horse?"

Joey looked at Fury, then back at Jim. "I'm sorry, Jim. I know I shouldn't have done it, but I felt awful. I chased Angel away because I couldn't stand it anymore."

Jim moved to the edge of the bed and put his arm around the boy's shoulders. "Okay, son," he said gently, "so you made a mistake. We all make them. Sometimes they're so serious they can't be corrected. Fortunately, this one can be."

Joey brightened. "You mean you're going to bring Angel back?"

"Only if you want her back. Do you?"

"Yes, I really do."

"How do you explain your sudden change of heart?"

"I don't know. Maybe it's because she does so much for Fury."

"And Fury can do no wrong, is that it?"

Joey nodded. "Can you and Pete ride out today and find her?"

"I'm afraid not. The blacksmith's coming, and we'll be busy all day rounding up our stock for him to shoe. It's a two-day job."

"You mean you can't go tomorrow, either?"

"No, not until the day after tomorrow."

"But what about Fury? What if he gets upset and runs away?"

"You'll have him at school most of the day. And just for these few nights, we'll lock him up."

"He'll hate that."

"I know, but think how happy he'll be when Angel finally does come back." Jim looked at his watch. "Now wash up, hop into your clothes, and come to breakfast."

Pete was pacing the floor as Jim came out into the living room. "Wal, how'd it go?" he asked anxiously.

"Simmer down, friend, everything's under control. He admitted his error and really regrets it."

Pete wiped his brow. "That's a relief. Say, Jim, that aunt of yours has been frettin' her head off. I tole her about Joey lettin' Angel out, an' about you goin' into his room fer a showdown. She was skeered you was goin' to whale the tar outa him, so she pranced right to the kitchen to cook him a stack of flapjacks."

"Good for her."

"That don't make no sense to me. How in tarnation kin flapjacks cure a stingin' sit-me-down?"

"A boy's favorite breakfast can make him forget lots of things, Pete. As it turned out, though, I didn't have to whale the tar out of him."

"I'm glad, 'cause I was mighty worried myself. What went on in Joey's room, anyways?"

"Come along to the kitchen, so I won't have to repeat myself."

In the kitchen, Jim related the whole story to Aunt Maggie and Pete. When Joey appeared for breakfast he finished the meal quickly and asked to be excused.

"What's your hurry?" asked Jim. "You don't usually leave for school this early."

"I know, but — well — I want Fury to take it easy today. If I don't race him and get him all excited, maybe he'll stay calm tonight and won't have to be locked up."

"Sorry, Joey, but he's going to be locked up tonight whether he seems calm or not. We can't leave him in the open after dark until we get Angel back."

"Okay," Joey said. "Good-bye, everybody."

A few minutes later he rode Fury through the gate and turned north on the trail that led to the schoolhouse. A quarter of a mile farther on, he left the trail and started westward across the meadow. Fury snorted and turned back toward the school trail.

Joey jerked the rein and brought him to the meadow again. "I know, Fury, it seems funny to leave the trail, but we're not going to school today. We're going to ride up and find Angel."

When the telephone rang at noon, Aunt Maggie was alone in the house.

"Is this the Broken Wheel Ranch?" the caller asked.

"Yes. This is Miss Newton speaking."

"How do you do, Miss Newton? I'm Helen Miller, Joey's schoolteacher."

"Oh yes, I've heard Joey speak of you many times. I'm looking forward to meeting you."

"Thank you. Perhaps we'll arrange that very soon. Miss Newton, I'm calling to ask about Joey. Is he ill today?"

Aunt Maggie stiffened. "Isn't he in school?"

"No, and he's so seldom absent I thought I'd better call and inquire about him." Helen Miller waited a moment. "Miss Newton, are you still on the line?"

"I'm sorry; I was thinking. Joey left for school this morning, shortly before his regular time."

"Oh dear. Did he say he was going to stop off anywhere?"

"No. Miss Miller, have you asked any of his classmates whether or not they've seen him?"

"Yes, but none of them had. I'm sorry to cause you anxiety, but I'm sure you understand why I'm calling."

"Of course, and I'm grateful to you. Now, if you'll excuse me, I must talk to my nephew."

"Very well. I'm sure there's some simple explanation for Joey's absence. Good-bye."

Aunt Maggie threw a shawl across her shoulders and hurried to the barn, where the blacksmith had set up his portable forge. Taking Jim and Pete aside, she told them about Miss Miller's call.

Jim looked grave. "I should've guessed it. Knowing Joey, I should've guessed he'd do this."

"Do what?" asked Aunt Maggie.

"I oughta guessed it, too," said Pete. "That boy's so all-fired anxious to make up fer what he done, he jest took off without tellin' us."

Aunt Maggie raised her voice. "But what did he do? Where did he go? I wish one of you would please tell me."

"He rode up to look for Angel," said Jim bluntly.

"By himself? Good gracious!"

"Good gracious ain't the half of it," said Pete. "If Angel went back to that same herd, Joey might run into that brown mustang stallion. An' that critter's a monster on four legs."

"In that case," said Aunt Maggie, "what're you two standing around for?"

"We're not," said Jim. "Saddle up, Pete." He looked toward the forge, where the blacksmith was shaping a white-hot shoe on the anvil. "Aunt Maggie, can you help the smith?"

"Certainly I can. Get going."

He squeezed her arm. "Good girl."

A few minutes later the men were riding hard.

At the water hole, Joey dismounted and examined the ground. According to all indications, the herd had left not long before.

"Take a drink, Fury, and let's get going."

Fury leaned down and took several deep draughts, then jerked his head up and turned southwest. Joey's shoulder was showered with water from the dripping muzzle. Climbing into the saddle again, he flipped the rein and gave Fury his head.

"You find Angel; you know where she is."

Fury started down the narrow trail which had been beaten hard over the years by the hoofs of many thirsty mustangs. It was the trail that Jim and Pete had taken the day they captured Angel. Fury followed it downward as it wound toward the flatland, his ears thrown forward and his nostrils quivering. As a sudden gust of wind lifted the russet leaves from the forest floor, he came to a dead stop and swiveled his head to the right.

"What is it?" Joey asked, in a half-whisper.

At the sound of the voice, Fury brought one ear around, then turned and dashed up the slope. Joey bent forward as the bare branches lashed his face. Another blast of wind blew down from the uplands, whipping the leaves into the air. Fury quickened his pace up the steady rise. Presently the trees grew farther apart, and Joey glimpsed bright sunlight in the distance. Realizing that he was approaching a clearing, he stared ahead, hoping to see the mustangs. As he rode into the open, he saw them, a large herd of mares huddled together for safety on the far side of the clearing. Angel stood on the near side of the group, her tail twitching, her eyes fixed upon Fury.

Joey felt his heart pounding, as he snatched his rope from the pommel and built a loop. As Fury dashed forward, all the mares but Angel wheeled and ran into the forest. The white mare stood her ground bravely, and Joey could see her body trembling. She watched the loop coming as he threw it, and made no move to free herself as it tightened about her neck.

Joey slid to the ground and ran up the rope. As he reached Angel's head, he was startled by an angry scream behind him, followed by a rumble of pounding hoofs. Whirling quickly, he saw the brown stallion emerging from the woods and coming toward him. With a cry of fear he darted behind Angel, as the sharp hoofs of the stallion raked the air, only inches from his head.

Now another fearful sound echoed through the forest, as Fury shrieked his battle challenge. From beneath the curve of Angel's neck, Joey saw Fury racing toward the wild stallion like a dark streak. Screaming a challenge of his own, the stallion turned in mid-air and charged to meet his attacker.

"Fury!" Joey cried. "Look out!"

As the animals crashed into each other, the ground shook beneath their weight. Rising to their hind legs, they lashed out with their forefeet, whistling shrilly. Fury lowered his head, and the mustang made a sudden move toward his throat. But Fury leaped aside in the nick of time, and the knife-edged teeth snapped together on thin air.

Thrown off balance, the mustang staggered, and as he struggled to regain his equilibrium, Fury whirled and lashed out with his hind legs. The hoofs struck the brown stallion in his left foreleg. With a shriek of pain and a dazed look in his eyes, he gave up the battle and limped into the woods. Giving a deep bellow of triumph, Fury followed him to the edge of the clearing.

"No!" Joey screamed. "Fury! Come back!"

As Fury glanced uncertainly at Joey, Angel whinnied.

With an answering whinny, Fury trotted to her side, puffing like an engine.

"You were great!" Joey cried. "You beat him!"

A low rumble came from the stallion's throat. Angel stepped forward and nibbled his ear.

"And now," Joey said, "let's take Angel home."

When he reached the flatland, with Angel trailing at the end of the rope, Jim and Pete spied him and rode up with joyous whoops. As they cantered homeward, Joey told them the story of Fury's battle.

"What a horse!" Pete said. "I won't see a better one till I git to heaven."

Jim reached out and placed his hand on Joey's

arm. "Fury risked his life to save you. Do you still believe he doesn't give a darn for you?"

Joey bent forward and covered Fury's ears with his hands. "Don't say that, Jim, he might hear you."

Chapter 8

DOC AND AUNT MAGGIE

Late one Friday afternoon, at the end of the first week of November, Doc Beemis, the medicine peddler, drove his battered truck through the gate of the BW and chugged up the hill to the house. Joey and Packy, who had been raking leaves, saw him and came running, with Crosby barking at their heels.

"Hi, Doc," Joey said cheerfully. "We expected you last month. You said you were coming back in October."

Doc reached over the door of the truck and shook Joey's hand. "That's quite true, Joseph. I did plan to return to this glorious ranch a trifle earlier, but I was detained by a short side excursion to Topeka, Kansas." He looked at Packy. "And who is this upstanding young lad? I don't seem to recall having seen his shining face before."

"This is Packy Lambert. Packy, this is our friend Doc Beemis."

111

"Pleased to meet you, Doctor," said Packy.

"I'm honored, Mr. Lambert," Doc answered politely.

Crosby, who had been sniffing the rear tires of the truck, came around to the driver's side and looked up. When Doc saw his old dog, he seemed pleased.

"Upon my word if it isn't Crosby, my erstwhile companion of the highways and byways. My arms have been aching to embrace this noble canine."

He opened the door and put one leg out. Crosby snarled and snapped at Doc's trouser cuff. Doc pulled the leg in hurriedly and slammed the door.

"Bless my soul, what a gruesome welcome!"

"Hey, Crosby!" Packy shouted. "Cut that out! I'm sorry he nipped at you, Doctor."

"I share your sorrow," said Doc, with a sigh. " 'How sharper than a serpent's tooth it is to have a thankless child!' "

"Why don't you get out of the truck, Doc?" Joey asked.

Doc Beemis cast a baleful glance at Crosby, who was eyeing him with his teeth bared.

"I'd like nothing better, Joseph. But this snarling carnivore seems to be lying in wait to rend me limb from limb."

"I can't understand why he's acting this way," Packy said. "He must be sick or something."

"An excellent diagnosis," said Doc. "What have you been feeding this dog, Joseph?"

"Nothing. He isn't mine anymore. He lives at Packy's house."

"In that case, I think young Mr. Lambert should

take him home at once and administer a healing medicine. In my professional opinion, this unfortunate canine is suffering from a slight touch of animus maximus."

"What's that?" asked Packy.

"A rare disease that can be cured quickly, but only at home. I suggest you take him there promptly so that I can get out of this vehicle."

Packy looked at Joey. "Do I have to go?"

"I think you'd better. Come back tomorrow."

"Okay. Come on, Crosby."

"One moment, lad." Doc Beemis opened a large medicine case and extracted a bottle of green liquid. "As a reward for your leaving so willingly, I should like to present you with a gift which will restore your mongrel — I mean your noble dog — to health."

"Gee, thanks," said Packy, examining the bottle. "What is it?"

"A secret formula manufactured from gnarled roots found only in Aztec ruins. It is known the world over as Beemis' Botanic Blood Balm. Your dear mother may find it useful also, for killing rodents."

"Boy, that's great," said Packy. "Come on, Crosby, let's go."

After Packy and Crosby had left, Doc stepped down from the truck and walked about stiffly. He was curious to learn the reason why Packy now owned the dog, and Joey explained.

"I never had a chance to thank you for giving me my ten dollars and forty-eight cents back," he concluded. "It was darn nice of you."

"Piffle," said Doc. "Don't give it a second thought." He glanced toward the house. "Where are James and Peter this afternoon?"

"Out in the east pasture repairing a fence. They'll be back pretty soon."

Doc took a small scuffed suitcase from the front seat. "Before they arrive, I wonder if you will extend me the courtesy of a basin of warm water and a thimble of soap flakes. I have a few dainty garments in this valise that could do with a bit of rinsing."

"Sure, come on. You can use my bathroom."

While Doc was doing his laundry, Joey sat on the edge of the tub, asking questions about his summer experiences.

"I traveled through eight of our sovereign states," Doc said, "stopping at each county, village, and farm. Everywhere I went I received my customary warm welcome. And when it came time to say farewell, I left with blessings and good wishes, plus a few bank notes and some small change."

"Did you cure anybody of anything?"

Doc was shocked by the question. "Did I *cure* anybody? My dear Joseph, I left a trail of miraculous cures that will be spoken of in hushed tones for centuries to come. Where shall I hang these wet socks?"

"On the shower-curtain rod. Here, I'll do it."

Joey looked at the socks and whistled. "Boy, these sure need darning. Don't you have a needle and thread?"

Doc shook his head.

"But your socks are full of holes. Maybe Aunt Maggie will darn them for you."

"Aunt Maggie? Who, pray tell, is she?"

"Jim's aunt from Philadelphia. Her name's Newton, too. She's been here since August."

"Do tell. Is the lady staying permanently?"

Joey hesitated. "Well, she said she was coming for just a couple of weeks. But I guess she likes it, because she's still here. And Jim can't ask her to leave because she's his aunt and it wouldn't be polite."

"A good woman on the premises can be both a jewel and an asset," said Doc. "What is your personal reaction to Aunt Maggie's continued presence?"

"Well, it's kind of hard to say. I like her but — well — we always had pretty good times together before she came. I don't mean I want her to leave, but, gosh, I don't know what I mean."

"A most informative answer. Can she cook?"

"Boy, I'll say she can."

"Hm, sounds like a fascinating woman. I look forward to meeting her."

"She's interested in you, too. I told her all about you. Come on, she's out in the kitchen."

"One moment, while I make myself presentable." Doc smoothed his eyebrows with his fingers. "Ah, that's better. Shall I bring my socks?"

"Later," said Joey, "when they're dry."

They found Aunt Maggie in the kitchen, making chicken soup.

"What a delectable aroma," Doc said, in an unusually loud voice, as they entered. "It stimulates the gastric juices in a most phenomenal fashion."

Aunt Maggie turned, saw Doc, and pushed back a strand of hair.

"Look who's here," said Joey. "Doc Beemis."

"Well," said Aunt Maggie pleasantly, "I'm delighted to meet you. Joey has told me a great deal about you."

Doc bowed from the waist and kissed her hand. "The pleasure is mine, Miss Newton. While I've been tidying up, Joey has been singing your praises."

Aunt Maggie glanced at her hand and seemed a trifle confused. "I'm afraid I'm not very presentable. I had no idea you were coming."

"No improvement could possibly be made," said Doc gallantly. "Your appearance is delightful. Do I smell chicken soup?"

"Why yes. I use an old recipe of my mother's."

"Look," Joey interrupted, "while you're talking, I'll go tell Jim and Pete Doc's here."

"Splendid," said Doc. "Miss Newton and I will converse while you're gone."

Joey found the men in the pasture, piling their tools into a pickup truck. "Doc Beemis is here!" he announced excitedly.

"That's great," said Jim. "We haven't seen him since February."

Pete chuckled. "How is the ole fraud? Still spoutin' hot air?"

"Sure, you know Doc. And guess what? He kissed Aunt Maggie's hand."

"He done *what?*"

"He kissed her hand. No kidding, just like in the movies."

"Wal, I'll be dadgummed. How'd she take it?"

"It upset her a little, I guess. She kind of blushed."

Jim was amused. "I'll bet that's the first time she's ever had her hand kissed. I'd like to have seen that."

"Me, too," said Pete. "That woulda been a sight."

Jim tossed a sledge hammer onto the truck. "Okay, Pete, we'll put these tools away, then go and see Doc."

The old man rubbed his chin thoughtfully. "Wait a second, Jim. Stick around a bit."

"What's the matter?"

"I'm thinkin'." He thought a moment longer, then snapped his fingers. "Hey, I got an idee! Jee-hosha-phat, what an idee!"

"What about?" asked Joey.

"Don't rush me." Pete turned to Jim. "Jim, I ain't bothered you for a long time about your aunt stayin' on here. But me an' her's had plenty of spats we ain't tole you about."

"Thanks for keeping them to yourself. I've had enough troubles around here without hearing about yours."

"Now I'm goin' to talk real plain, Jim, an' I want you to listen."

"Go ahead."

"This aunt of yours has been here since August, an' now it's November. If she don't pack up an' leave soon, she'll be here forever."

"Look," said Jim wearily, "if you're going to tell me to ask her to leave you're wasting your breath."

"But I ain't tellin' you that." Pete thrust his chin out and looked Jim straight in the eye. "Do you want that woman to stay forever? Wal, tell me, do you?"

Jim sighed. "No, Pete, of course I don't, but . . ."

Pete turned to Joey. "What about you? Do *you* want her to stay on this ranch forever? Don't fib now; tell me the honest truth."

"Well, no, not forever, but . . ."

"There, you see?" cried Pete triumphantly. "Now all three of us know jest where we stand."

"What're you getting at, Pete?" asked Jim.

Pete giggled like a schoolboy. "A plot, that's what I'm gittin' at. A plot to git Aunt Maggie to leave without you askin' her to."

Joey frowned. "A plot?"

"Yep. Now listen an' I'll tell you what it is. The whole thing hinges on Doc Beemis." Pete glanced over his shoulder toward the house and lowered his voice. "When Doc was here in February he told us that he was lookin' fer a wife, right?" Jim and Joey nodded. "Okay. A minute ago Joey said Doc kissed Aunt Maggie's hand an' she turned red, right?"

"That's right," said Joey.

Pete spread his arms out. "Wal? Now is it plain to you what I'm gittin' at? If it ain't, yer both blockheads."

Jim laughed. "You old scoundrel. I never would have believed that you'd turn out to be a matchmaker."

"But it makes good sense, don't it?"

"Wait a second," Joey said. "Do you mean Doc might ask Aunt Maggie to marry him or something crazy like that?"

"Exac'ly!"

Jim climbed into the truck and started the motor. "While you two are cooking up a movie romance,

118

I'm going to put these tools away. See you at the house."

"The thing to do," said Pete, after Jim had driven off, "is to keep tellin' Doc Beemis what a wonderful woman Aunt Maggie is. You keep tellin' him an' I'll keep tellin' him."

"But you hate Aunt Maggie. You'd be lying."

"So what? Tellin' a few fibs wouldn't be no sin if it brought two people together, would it?"

"Well, no, I guess it wouldn't, if it made them happy."

"Right." Pete rubbed his hands together. "C'mon. Let's go up an' give that ole coot a sales talk."

The sales talk had to be put off for an hour, because Doc Beemis wouldn't leave the kitchen. He seemed to be settled there forever, as he related his summer adventures to Aunt Maggie and the men. Pete made many attempts to get him outdoors, but he just stayed there, talking a blue streak.

"The Swamp Root was my best seller in Missouri," said Doc. "But in Colorado the Magic Nerve Beans went like hot cakes. On the other hand, the good people of Nebraska fought tooth and nail to purchase Dromgoole's English Bitters."

"What are they for?" asked Aunt Maggie, fascinated.

"Chest pains, gout, and ague, my dear. There's nothing more effective in the entire catalogue of materia medica."

"An' Doc oughta know," said Pete to Aunt Maggie. "He's one of the smartest men I ever met."

"What other things were you selling this summer?" Joey asked.

"My usual line of reliable and time-tested products. Electric Plasters, Ozmantis Oriental Pills, Prickly Ash Bitters, Shiloh's Vitalizer, Tansy Capsules, Peruna, and Mother's Friend. I also carried a small stock of pots and pans."

"Speakin' of pots an' pans," said Pete, "Jim's aunt here is one of the finest cooks this side of Chicago."

Aunt Maggie was stunned by Pete's praise. "What a lovely compliment. Thank you, Pete."

Jim moved to the door. "I've got to wash up. You'll stay for dinner, won't you, Doc?"

"I will indeed, James. After Peter's glowing tribute to Miss Newton's culinary accomplishments, wild horses couldn't drag me away."

"We'd be delighted to have you," said Aunt Maggie.

"You're too kind, my dear."

"Wal," said Pete, taking Doc's arm, "let's you an' Joey an' me mosey down an' see Fury."

"Now?" asked Doc.

Pete tightened his grasp. "Yep, right now."

Before Doc could say another word, Pete had hastened him through the kitchen door. As they were walking toward the corral, Pete gave Joey a nudge with his elbow.

"Start talkin'," he muttered. "Lay it on thick."

Joey nodded and winked. "Say, Doc," he began, "uh, how do you like Aunt Maggie? Isn't she the greatest?"

"Indeed she is, Joseph. Fine woman, splendid character."

"And what a cook! Man!"

"An' when it comes to housekeepin'," said Pete,

"there ain't a woman in the state that kin touch her. Not a speck of dust, anywheres. You could eat off the floor."

"A strange place to partake of food," said Doc dryly.

"In a manner of speakin', I mean," Pete added quickly. "We got the shiniest table an' the whitest tablecloth you ever laid eyes on."

"How is the lady's disposition?" Doc asked. "That, I find, is a most important factor."

"She's the easygoin'est, sweet-temperedest female that ever lived. Matter of fact, I wisht I'd met up with her when I was a little younger."

"Oh, brother!" Joey whispered, trying hard not to laugh.

Pete gave him a poke in the ribs. "Hush up, we got him interested."

"Ah," said Doc, as they reached the corral, "here is my old friend Fury, the noblest stallion of them all. And who is the white beauty standing at his side?"

"That's Angel," said Joey.

"Lookit the two of 'em standin' so close together," said Pete. "Fury was on'y half a horse till this little mare come to keep him comp'ny. An' that's jest the way it oughta be. No man or animal kin reely find happiness, till he finds somebody to share it with."

Doc looked at Pete in amazement. "A great change has come over you, Peter, and I'm delighted. You've always been a cantankerous old buzzard, but now you've softened into something almost human. What brought it about?"

"Aunt Maggie," Pete answered with a straight

face. "I ain't never had the influence of a good woman before."

"Neither have I," Joey added truthfully. "Everything on the ranch is better since Aunt Maggie came."

"Let's hope she never leaves us," Pete said. "I'm skeered all the time she might take a shine to some feller an' marry him. If that ever happens, we'll shore be lost at the BW, but of course the bridegroom'd be the luckiest galoot in the world."

As Doc leaned over the fence to scratch Angel's head, Joey whispered into Pete's ear. "You'd better ease up a little. You're laying it on too thick."

When dinner was announced, Doc Beemis was the first one at the table. With his napkin tucked into his collar, he watched Aunt Maggie eagerly as she brought in the food. She was wearing her company dress, which had lace on it, and was made of silk that rustled when she walked.

The dinner, as Doc Beemis described it, was "a culinary masterpiece, executed by a genius." He was so obviously pleased by the food that Pete found it unnecessary to add any extravagant praise of his own. After each flowery comment delivered by Doc, Aunt Maggie beamed.

Jim, who had scoffed at the idea of a romance between his aunt and Doc, now realized that perhaps there might be something to it after all, and watched the proceedings with genuine interest.

At the end of the meal, Aunt Maggie's special after-dinner coffee was served in the living room. Doc Beemis, who had accepted an invitation to stay overnight, settled himself in a comfortable chair close to the crackling fire. Aunt Maggie took the other upholstered chair and easily assumed the role of hostess. Finally, as so often happens in ranch country, the subject turned to the West of long ago.

"I've always been fascinated by the men and women who opened this country," Jim said, looking into the fire. "The fur traders, the land-hungry settlers, the gold-seeking Forty-niners, and the men who built the railroads that brought the East and West together."

"It woulda been real excitin' to live in them days," Pete said.

Aunt Maggie spoke up. "When I was a little girl, my grandfather used to tell me stories about *his* grandfather's wagon-train journey in 1806, from Pennsylvania to Ontario, Canada. It's strange how certain things stand out so vividly in my memory: an Indian attack; a broken axle; a frantic search for food; and a stormy trip on a raft across Lake Ontario, with animals and wagons. Joey, I'm sure you'd be interested in hearing how they made butter along the way."

"I sure would. How did they do it?"

"They hung pails of cream to the rear axles of their wagons, and after a day's jouncing the cream turned into butter."

Doc Beemis grinned. "I must remember that, Miss Newton. The way my old truck bounces, I could manufacture a pailful of butter every two miles."

"We have lots of books here about the Old West," Joey said. "The one I like best is the life of Jim Bridger. He was a great Indian fighter and wagon-train leader, but, boy, what whoppers he told. The funniest one was how he turned an echo into an alarm clock."

Pete leaned forward. "Whattya mean? How's such a thing possible?"

"Well, he often stopped for the night at a certain camping ground on the edge of a valley. On the other side of the valley there was a high mountain. But it was so far away that the echo from any sound made in the camp didn't come back for six hours. So Jim Bridger used the echo as an alarm clock. Before he went to sleep at night he'd call out, 'Time to get up!', and six hours later the echo would come back and wake him."

"A disgraceful exaggeration," Doc Beemis said piously. "I could never cotton to a man who distorts the truth. And neither could my grandfather, Nicodemus Beemis." He shook his head. "There was one man to whom the truth was sacred. When he told a story, you could be certain it actually happened. Especially his bear-hunting story."

When Doc didn't continue, Joey became curious. "What was his bear-hunting story?"

"I doubt that I should tell it to you, Joseph, because you'd think it was a tall tale. Everyone does, more's the pity."

"Oh, come on, Doc, let's hear it."

Doc gave in. "Well, if you insist, I suppose I must. Nicodemus Beemis was a hunter *par excellence*. One day, as he was stalking a moose through the forest, he saw a giant bear raise its head from behind a log not far ahead. Nicodemus took aim, fired, and saw the bear fall. As he started forward toward the log, the bear raised its head again. Nicodemus fired a second shot, and again the bear fell. The bear's head appeared three times more, and each time the mighty hunter shot it down. After he had fired five shots in all, he walked up to the log, looked over, and saw a sight that no hunter had ever seen before."

"What'd he see?" asked Joey.

"Five dead bears."

As everyone laughed, Doc shook his head sadly. "I knew you wouldn't believe that tale. I never should have told it."

When the clock struck ten, Aunt Maggie stood up. "If you'll excuse me, I'd better see to the dinner dishes. You stay right here and enjoy yourselves."

Doc Beemis pushed himself up from his comfortable chair. "Nonsense, my dear lady. I won't hear of your attacking that miserable chore all alone. Allow me to assist you."

"Thank you, but it really isn't necessary."

"Tush," said Doc. "It's high time I learned the art of dish-washing and similar domestic skills. Such knowledge will stand me in good stead in the near future."

"We'll all come out and lend a hand," Jim called, as Doc and Aunt Maggie disappeared into the kitchen. "Come on, Joey. You, too, Pete."

"Wait a second," said Pete, in a low voice that trembled with excitement. "Let them two have a little time together without us. I think Doc's goin' to pop the question."

"You mean ask her to marry him?" said Joey.

"Shore."

Jim laughed. "There you go again, building up a romance."

Pete was insistent. "But didn't you hear what he said? He said it's high time he learned dishwashin' an' stuff like that, fer somethin' that might happen in the near future. This is it, fellas! There's goin' to be a weddin', or I'm a cross-eyed hoot owl."

"Well, you'd better learn to hoot," Jim said, "because you might be in for a disappointment. Now come on, let's all go to the kitchen and pitch in."

With five people working, the dishes were finished in no time. As they worked, Pete watched Doc and Aunt Maggie closely for some sign that they had been drawn to each other. When no such sign appeared, he felt that time was running out and that he'd better do something about it.

"Say, Jim," he said casually, "seein' it's Friday night, how about askin' Doc to stay fer the weekend?"

"That would be fine. How are you fixed for food, Aunt Maggie?"

"There's plenty of everything, Jim. On Sunday night perhaps we could have a barbecue."

"That'd be great," said Joey. "How about it, Doc, will you stay?"

Doc shook his head. "I'm flattered by the invitation, and under different circumstances I would accept instantly. However, fate has decreed that I must rise early tomorrow morning and start my lengthy journey to Topeka, Kansas."

Pete saw his hopes fading. "I heerd we're goin' to have a bad storm tomorrow, Doc. Let's go outside an' have a look at the sky. If it looks like snow, you better put off yer leavin' till Monday."

As they stepped into the open, Doc glanced upward. "It's clear as a bell, Peter; never seen such a perfect night. I think I shall get under way immediately after breakfast."

"Look," Pete said bluntly, "let's talk turkey. Whattya think of Aunt Maggie?"

"She is a perfect jewel."

"Does that mean you like her a lot?"

"I find her utterly charming. And kindly stop clawing at my sleeve; this garment isn't made of iron."

"The heck with yer sleeve; let's talk about you an' Aunt Maggie. How about it?"

"How about what?"

"Don't act so dumb," Pete snapped. "When you was here last February didn't you say you was lookin' fer a sensible woman to take care of you in yer old age?"

"I did say that, Peter; I did indeed. And that is precisely why I'm impatient to begin my journey to Topeka. There's someone waiting there to greet me."

"Who?"

"Mrs. Beemis."

"Yer mother?"

"No, my dear friend, my wife. A month ago I was lawfully wedded to the fairest flower in the state of Kansas, and she's pining for my return."

Pete shuffled back into the house, a dazed and beaten man.

"What's wrong with you?" Jim asked. "You look like a ghost."

Aunt Maggie led Pete to a chair. "You'd better sit down."

"What happened?" Joey asked. "You look as if you just got some terrible news."

Pete stared at the floor. "I did. Doc tole me he got hitched last month to a gal in Topeka."

"Heaven help her," said Aunt Maggie. "Doc's amusing, but I can't imagine any woman in her right mind ever wanting to marry him. He's an old windbag." She waved her hand daintily. "Well, good night all. I'll see you in the morning."

Chapter 9
THE FBI STEPS IN

Toward the middle of November, when bitter night winds blew down from the mountains, it was decided that Angel and Fury should sleep indoors. The time for the birth of Angel's foal was six or seven weeks away, and everyone looked forward eagerly to the newcomer's arrival. Two stalls were constructed in a small outbuilding behind the main barn, so that Fury and his mate could rest comfortably and undisturbed.

Since Angel had come to the Broken Wheel Ranch to stay, Joey had thought less frequently about Mr. Yancey's threat to destroy Fury if anyone reported his timber rustling; and when the stallion began sleeping indoors at night, Joey had forgotten about it almost entirely.

Yancey's theft of timber, owned by the United States government, went undiscovered by any person in authority until the Tuesday before Thanksgiving. That morning, a forest ranger named Al Kenyon flew over the area in a helicopter, noted that many acres of timber had been cut illegally, and reported the theft to the Bureau of Land Management. Later in the day, a BLM investigator discussed the case with Harry Shroder, a special agent of the Federal Bureau of Investigation. The following morning, Kenyon and Shroder rode up to the area and verified the timber trespass. Satisfied that Yancey was the only possible suspect, they proceeded to his home and arrested him on a charge of theft of government property.

At the county seat the indignant lumberman at first denied the charge, but after constant questioning he broke down and sullenly admitted his guilt. After posting bail of one thousand dollars, he was released from custody.

"It was that kid," he muttered angrily to Kenyon. "If that nosy kid hadn't tipped you off, nobody would've ever found out about it."

"What kid?" Kenyon asked.

"Never mind, forget it."

"Look," the ranger assured him, "nobody tipped me off. I found out about it myself, during a routine investigation."

"Sure, sure, anything you say."

Kenyon shook his head as Yancey mounted his horse and rode away. In all his experience, the forest ranger had never seen a man so close to bursting with pent-up rage.

That night Yancey paced the floor of his cabin, planning vengeance upon Joey, through Fury.

* * *

On Thanksgiving night, Packy's parents, Chris and Stella Lambert, gave a giant supper party, followed by square dancing in the barn. Neighbors for miles around were invited to attend; and a fiddler, a guitarist, and a banjo player were engaged to supply the music.

The week before the party, Chris dropped in at the Broken Wheel to ask Pete to do him a favor.

"Stella and I have been wondering who we'd get to call the figures for the square dance, and we decided that you'd do the job beautifully. How about it, Pete?"

"Me?" said Pete in amazement. "You must be off yer noodle."

"Why do you say that?"

" 'Cause I ain't called a dance in years."

"Maybe so," Chris argued, "but some old-timers in this valley tell me you're an expert."

"Bushwa. They must be off their noodles, too."

"No, they know what they're talking about, and they say you're the ideal man for the job. So come on, Pete, don't let us down. Say you'll do it."

The old man toed the ground. "Aw shucks, Chris, I'd on'y end up by makin' a danged ole fool of meself." He pointed to Jim. "Why not let him do the callin'? He's real good at it."

Jim threw his hands up. "Not on your life. I'm not the expert, you are. Besides, the caller never gets a chance to dance with the ladies, and I want to get Aunt Maggie out there on the floor."

Pete wrinkled his nose. "Aunt Maggie? Is she invited?"

"Of course," said Chris. "She's going to be one of our honored guests."

"Okay," said Pete, with a shrug. "In that case I'll take the job. If I'm goin' to be up on the platform all evenin', I won't hafta dance with her."

"Thanks," Chris said, "that's a big load off my mind."

"What time do you want us there?" Jim asked.

"Five o'clock will be fine. There's going to be a big crowd, so come early."

"We'll be there on the dot."

Late Thanksgiving afternoon everybody at the BW got dressed in his best, in preparation for the party.

"You look mighty pretty," Jim told Aunt Maggie, as she came into the living room. "I wouldn't be surprised if you turned out to be the belle of the ball."

Aunt Maggie blushed. "Oh go along with you. Who'd look at me?"

"Plenty of people."

"Who, for instance?"

"Well," Jim said teasingly, "there'll be lots of handsome bachelors and widowers there, and I'll bet they flock around you like flies around the sugar bowl."

"You and your blarney. Honestly, you sound more like Doc Beemis than Jim Newton."

Pete came from his room, dressed in new pants, shiny new boots, and a bright green shirt tied at the neck with an orange kerchief.

"Wow!" said Jim, covering his eyes. "That wild shirt almost blinds me."

"You think mebbe it's a mite too loud?" Pete said anxiously.

"Not at all. It's exactly what the well-dressed square dance caller's wearing this season."

"You look just grand," said Aunt Maggie.

Pete stole a glance at his reflection in the wall mirror. "Thank you kindly. If you both think it's okay, I guess I'll keep it on."

"Joey," Jim called, "aren't you almost ready? I'm about to bring the car around."

"Okay," answered Joey, coming from his room. "Boy, don't we all look fancy!"

While Jim was getting the car, Joey ran out to the small barn to check on Fury and Angel. Satisfied that they were warm and comfortable, he joined the others at the car and they set out for the Lamberts'.

The barn was decorated with cornstalks, pumpkins, and colored lights, and the guests were seated on bales of straw at long trestle tables. Aunt Maggie, either by chance or by design, was placed between Mr. Barstow, who was a widower, and a middle-aged bachelor named Gene Lowell. Throughout supper, both men kept her busy with conversation, and it was obvious that she was having a great time.

Later, while the tables were being cleared away and the platform for the musicians set up, Pete drew Jim and Joey aside.

"Lookit Aunt Maggie," he said in a conspirator's voice. "Looks like she's havin' herself a real good time."

"She's about as popular as anybody in the barn," said Jim.

Pete winked. "I been watchin' her all through

supper, an' if you ask me, she's got ole Barstow right smack in the palm of her hand."

"I hope so," Joey said. "He's a millionaire."

Jim laughed. "You sound like a couple of match-makers."

"I wish I could," said Pete. "Wouldn't it be great if we could git Aunt Maggie married off?"

Jim glanced at the platform. "You'd better save your voice, old-timer. The music's about ready to start, and you'll need it to call the figures."

"Don't you fret none about me runnin' outa voice. I been garglin' with vinegar an' water all afternoon."

When the musicians had their instruments tuned and ready, Pete climbed to the platform and called for attention.

"Okay, folks, the square dance is about to git started, so grab yer pardners an' take yer places! The first number on the program is that ole country fav'-rite, 'Frogs on a Lily Pad.' "

Giving a signal to the fiddler, Pete threw his head back and began calling the figures. At the end of the first tune, he slid right into the next one without seeming to take a breath. The moment he'd finished "Yelp an' Holler," he swung into "Gals in Calico," "Idaho Twist," and "Duck for the Apple," and fin-ished the set with "Grab for the Chicken Leg."

All during the calling he kept his eyes glued on Aunt Maggie, who was capering about the barn like a youngster. First she danced with Mr. Barstow; then she changed partners and danced in turn with Jim, Gene Lowell, and Al Kenyon, the forest ranger.

Shortly before ten o'clock, while Pete was still going at full steam, a man tethered his horse at the end of the road and walked stealthily toward the gaily lighted barn. Passing the long line of parked cars, he circled the building and peered through the large window at the rear. Shading his eyes with one hand, he searched the faces of the party guests until he had located Jim, Pete, and Joey. Satisfied that he would not be disturbed in the job that he was about to do, he returned to his horse and set out for the Broken Wheel Ranch.

The man was Mark Yancey.

When he arrived at the BW, the ranch house and outbuildings were in darkness. Dismounting at the door of the big barn, he slid the bolt, swung the door open, and went inside. With a flashlight he hurried past the stalls, shining the beam into the eyes of the startled horses. When he found that Fury was not among them, he swore softly and went outside. Sweeping his light in an arc, he presently discovered the small outbuilding behind the barn and ran toward it. He pushed the bolt back, then stepped through the door and raised his flashlight. Fury snorted as the bright glare blinded him momentarily. In the adjoining stall, Angel whinnied and backed up.

Yancey grunted with satisfaction, and put his light down on a sawhorse. Working quickly, he gathered a pile of dry straw in his arms and dropped it near the door. He retrieved his flashlight, stepped over the pile of straw, struck a match, and dropped it. Without waiting to slide the bolt of the outside door, he mounted his horse and galloped down the road. As he passed through the main gate, he looked back and saw a yellow glow behind the barn. By the time he had ridden a quarter of a mile onto the meadow, the glow had become a blaze.

At the Lamberts' party, Pete was just getting his second wind. As he called the figures for "Owl on the Corncrib," he noticed with pleasure that Aunt Maggie was dancing once again with Mr. Barstow. Catching Jim's eye, he pointed gleefully to the dancing couple. Jim grinned and turned away to talk to Al Kenyon.

"I haven't seen you for a long time, Al," Jim said. "What've you been doing with yourself?"

"Oh, I've been earning my pay." Kenyon saw Joey coming toward them. "Say, is this Joey? If it is, he's certainly sprouted up in a hurry."

"It's Joey, all right. Joey, you remember Al Kenyon, the forest ranger?"

"I sure do." Joey shook Kenyon's outstretched hand. "I saw you before, Mr. Kenyon, but didn't get a chance to talk to you."

"You're quite a dancer," said Kenyon. "I saw you doing the elbow swing with young Kathie Emerson. She's real nice."

"Yeah, but she's a whole year older than me."

"By the way, Al," said Jim, "a few days ago I saw a helicopter flying back and forth across the ridge. Were you flying it?"

"Yes, I thought I'd better take a look up there before winter sets in." Kenyon paused to light his pipe. "Lucky thing I did, too. I uncovered a timber trespass."

Joey felt the blood draining from his face. "You uncovered a what?"

"A timber trespass. I found out that a lumberman up there had been cutting government trees."

Joey turned away to conceal the fright that he knew was written on his face.

"Who was it?" Jim asked. "Anybody I know?"

"Maybe so. His name's Mark Yancey."

Joey whirled. "Mark Yancey?"

"Say, are you feeling all right?" Kenyon asked. "All of a sudden you look kind of pale."

"Joey's had a few run-ins with Yancey," Jim explained. "I guess that's why he seems so shocked."

"What happened to him?" Joey asked hoarsely. "Is he in jail?"

"He was yesterday, but only for a few hours. He was finally released on bail."

Joey's legs felt weak. "You mean, he's free?"

Jim slipped his arm under Joey's shoulders. "Joey! What's wrong?"

"Mr. Yancey! He said he'd — he'd kill Fury if anybody ever found out!"

"What're you talking about? Joey, tell me!"

Kenyon raised his hand. "Wait, Jim. Now I remember something Yancey said yesterday after he'd left the courthouse." He bent forward. "Joey, did you know Yancey had cut government trees?"

Joey turned his head away. "Why do you want to know?"

"Because he muttered something about a nosy kid tipping me off."

"But I *didn't* tip you off! I never told anybody!"

"Joey," said Jim sternly, "tell the truth! What happened? What're you keeping from us?"

There was a note of tragic despair in Joey's voice,

as he told the men the story of his discovery and of Yancey's threat to kill Fury if he were ever arrested for his crime.

"I'm sorry I lied to you, Jim," he concluded miserably. "But don't you see? I had to, to save Fury."

"We'll talk about that later. Meanwhile, there's no time to waste. Let's slip out of here without being seen. Al, I'd like you to come along."

Kenyon frowned. "Where to?"

"The BW. Come on, hurry!"

When the pile of straw burst into flame, Fury rose to his hind legs and kicked viciously at the door of his stall. Angel saw the fire and turned away, whinnying with terror. Fury glanced at her, then kicked again at the door. It flew open as the hook snapped in two. Rushing from his stall, he ran toward the burning straw and pranced about it uncertainly. A shrill cry from Angel brought him back to the front of her stall. The small building was filling with smoke, and as the mare cowered at the rear of her enclosure, she drew a deep breath and burst into a fit of coughing.

Although terrified by the flames that were licking at the door of the barn, Fury lowered his head and curled his lips back. With his strong teeth he lifted the hook that fastened Angel's stall, then thrust his head over the door, and swung it open with his chin. Giving a shrill, commanding whistle, he stepped backward, inviting Angel to come out. Hysterical with fear, the mare hugged the back wall of her stall. Glancing again at the flaming door, Fury stepped into the stall and took her left ear between his teeth.

She squealed with pain, and attempted to wriggle free; but Fury held on and backed up. When he had drawn her from the stall, though she was still protesting; he moved behind her and butted her toward the door of the barn.

Angel planted her forelegs on the floor and refused to budge, her frightened eyes fixed upon the blaze. Whirling quickly, Fury flung his hind legs out and raked her rump with his hoofs. With a cry of pain she sprang forward to avoid being kicked again, and leaped toward the flames. Her body crashed into the barn door, flinging it wide. As she ran into the open, gasping for air, Fury dashed through the blaze and came to her side.

The entire front wall of the small structure was burning, and as Angel looked back at it fearfully, Fury butted her toward the field behind the big barn, where they stood side by side, panting and trembling.

A half-mile from the ranch, as Jim's car turned off the wagon road, the riders saw a red glow in the sky to the north.

"There's a fire up there!" Kenyon exclaimed.

Joey leaned out over the door. "It's our place! Jim, it's the BW!"

Jim reached out and grabbed Joey's belt. "Sit down!"

The tires kicked up dust as Jim shoved the pedal to the floor. When they turned in at the gate, the ranch house and barn stood out in silhouette against the leaping flames.

"It's Fury's barn!" Joey wailed. "He'll be killed!"

Kenyon leaned forward in the back seat and took Joey by the collar. "Easy, son, easy."

Jim sat tight-lipped at the wheel, as the car roared up the road and stopped beside the big barn. All three leaped out at once and ran toward the blaze.

Jim caught Joey by the shoulder. "Stay back! The building's gone!"

"Fury!" Joey screamed. "Fury, where are you?"

Over the crackling of the flames they heard the stallion's answering cry. Turning toward the pasture, they saw his eyes reflected in the dancing light. Angel appeared as a snowy figure beside him. Shouting with relief, Joey ran into the field and threw his arms about Fury's quivering neck. Angel sidled up to him and nudged him with her muzzle.

"Oh, Fury!" Joey cried. "You got out! And you got Angel out, too!"

"Are they all right?" Jim called.

"Yes, but they're shivering."

"Take them to the big barn and rub them down. We'll try to keep this fire from spreading."

Joey led the horses into vacant stalls, while Jim and Kenyon broke out the pressure hose and played the stream of water on the crumbling structure.

"We're lucky the wind's blowing away from the other buildings," Kenyon shouted. "Otherwise you'd stand to lose the whole ranch."

After an hour of strenuous labor, the men were still pouring water on the smoking ruin. As Joey was about to leave the barn, the phone rang. It was Pete, calling from the Lambert place.

"What in tarnation're you doin' home?" he demanded angrily. "Don't you realize the dance is over, an' I'm trapped here with Aunt Maggie?"

Joey tried to explain, but the words rushed out so fast he made little sense.

"Hold on!" Pete roared through the receiver. "I can't make out a word yer sayin'! Put Jim on!"

"He can't come now; he's busy at the fire."

Joey heard the old man gasp at the other end of the line. "Fire? What fire?"

Again Joey started at the beginning. "The little barn. I'm sure Mr. Yancey set fire to it to kill Fury and . . ."

"Yancey done *what?*"

"Look," Joey said impatiently, "I've got to go out and help Jim and Mr. Kenyon."

"Kenyon? What's he doin' there?"

"I'll tell you later. You stay there with Aunt Maggie, and later we'll drive over and get you. G'bye."

"Wait!" Pete pleaded. "Don't hang up!"

"I've got to. So long."

A half-hour later, when one of the ranchers delivered Pete and Aunt Maggie to the house, Kenyon was at Jim's desk talking to FBI Agent Shroder on the telephone. Pete was in a sputtering rage, having been, as he put it, "deserted like rats leavin' a sinkin' ship." Jim took Pete and his aunt aside, and told them what had taken place.

Aunt Maggie was horrified. "It was monstrous! Simply monstrous!"

"It was worse than that," Joey said soberly. "Fury and Angel might've been killed."

Pete pounded the wall with his fist. "Why the heck din you bring me back with you, instead of leavin' me there makin' a dang fool of meself?"

"There was no time," said Jim. "Besides, we didn't want to ruin the party."

Aunt Maggie glanced at Kenyon. "Is he talking to the police?"

"No, the FBI agent."

Pete picked up the poker. "If I had my way, I'd git a posse together an' ride up to Yancey's place tonight!"

"Simmer down," said Jim. "So far, we have no definite proof that he started the fire."

"How much more do you need?" Pete demanded. "That Yancey oughta be strung up, that's what he oughta be!"

Kenyon finished his telephone call and joined the group. They looked at him questioningly.

"We're going to get some quick action," Kenyon said. "Harry Shroder's pretty well satisfied that Yancey started the fire to carry out his threat to Joey. Shroder and I are going to ride up there in the morning and arrest Yancey on suspicion of arson."

"Why not tonight?" Pete demanded.

"We'll need daylight, in case he decides to put up an argument." Kenyon turned to Jim. "Want to come along with us?"

"Thanks," said Jim impassively. "I'll be glad for your company."

"What do you mean?"

"If you and Shroder hadn't decided to go, I was going to go alone."

At nine in the morning, Jim, Kenyon, and Shroder left the skid road and turned their horses onto Yancey's property. The FBI agent turned in his saddle.

"Okay, this is it. Check your weapons and proceed as quietly as possible from here on."

Shroder took the lead, with Jim just behind him and Kenyon trailing. Listening intently, they threaded their way through the desolate waste of jagged stumps. There was no sound of logging in progress, and the area seemed deserted. When they came to the foot of the path leading up to the house, the FBI man gave the signal to dismount. Working silently, they tethered their horses and drew their rifles from the saddle holsters.

"Keep low," Shroder cautioned them, "and be ready to drop behind a stump if necessary."

In single file they crept up the path, using the trees for protection. Where the path curved, they saw the house.

"I'll cover the front door," Shroder whispered. "You two keep your eyes glued on those log cabins."

Twenty yards from the house, Shroder stood up and called Yancey's name. Receiving no answer, he called again. "Yancey! Yancey, are you in there?"

The men listened, but heard nothing.

"This is the FBI!" Shroder cried. "There are three of us here, and we're armed!"

Detecting a slight movement behind the shade that covered the glass door Shroder raised his weapon.

"All right, Yancey! Open the door and come out with your hands in the air!"

After a moment of dead silence, there came a sudden shattering of glass and a rifle barrel slid through the bottom of the broken pane. Shroder threw himself to the ground as the rifle cracked and a slug whined past his head.

"Hold your fire!" he yelled to the others, as he rolled behind a stump. "Don't shoot unless he comes out and tries to rush us!"

"Yancey!" Jim shouted. "This is Jim Newton. Don't be an idiot and get yourself killed! Come out and surrender!"

Yancey's voice rang out for the first time. "Come and get me, all three of you! I'll pick you off before you reach the steps!"

Shroder spoke in a low voice. "I'm going to work my way to the back of the house. You two cover me."

As he rose to a kneeling position, Yancey's rifle spat again. The lead thudded into the stump, showering him with splinters. Shroder fired from the hip, shattering the remaining glass above Yancey's head. Yancey stood outlined in the bare frame of the door, a bewildered expression on his face. The three men leaped to their feet, their rifles aimed directly at Yancey's head.

"Don't move!" Shroder commanded. "Just push your gun out the door!"

Yancey's eyes darted from Shroder to Kenyon to Jim. The cornered man seemed to be weighing his chances.

"Don't try it!" Jim called dryly. "Push your gun out!"

Yancey shrugged. "Okay, boys, anything you say."

His weapon clattered to the porch, and Shroder leaped up the steps and pounced on it. Jim and Kenyon followed him, their rifles still raised. Jim kicked the door open and grabbed Yancey by the collar.

"Don't shoot!" Yancey cried in sudden terror. "Don't!"

Jim yanked him roughly through the door and pushed him toward Shroder. "Take charge of him," he said disgustedly, "before I lose my temper."

The FBI agent took out a pair of handcuffs and snapped them around Yancey's wrists.

"Where's your horse?"

Yancey motioned with his head. "Back in the tool shed."

"I'll saddle him," Kenyon said.

"Hurry it up," said Shroder. "We've got a long ride to town — in pretty miserable company."

Chapter 10

AUNT MAGGIE'S MISTAKE

On the day of Yancey's capture, Joey had breathed a sigh of relief. The terrible burden of the lumberman's threat to kill Fury had been lifted forever.

"You'll never know how awful I felt," he told Jim. "I'd never lied to you before, and I used to worry about it in bed at night."

Jim was naturally sympathetic. "It was a frightening experience for you, Joey, but I think it taught you a valuable lesson. Whenever anyone is threatened with violence, they should report it immediately. If you'd told me about it, I would have gone straight to the police and we would have seen to it that Fury was protected."

"I know that now, Jim, but I was so scared he'd kill Fury I didn't dare tell anybody." Joey frowned. "But he almost did kill Fury — and Angel, too."

"Well, try to forget it," Jim said finally. "You'll never have to worry about Yancey again."

146

Joey walked to the window and looked toward the charred ruins of the small barn. "I guess there's always something for a fellow to worry about, though."

"Oh? What's upsetting you now?"

"Angel. She must've been frightened almost to death during the fire. Do you think her foal's going to be all right, when it comes?"

"Well, you heard what Doc Weathers said this afternoon, when he came out to examine her. He said it looks as though everything's going to be okay. And Doc should know what he's talking about; he's the best vet in this part of the state."

"When does he think the foal's going to be born?"

"In about four or five weeks."

Joey grinned. "Then Aunt Maggie was right. She said it would be late December or early January."

"She knows a great deal about horses, Joey. And about people, too. She's a rather remarkable woman."

"I know, and I like her a lot. But Pete doesn't. I think he really hates her."

"Oh, I don't think Pete really hates her; he just feels that he'd have more freedom if the three of us were here by ourselves, as we were before she came."

"It was kind of fun then," Joey said wistfully. "Don't you think it was, Jim?"

Jim hesitated. "Well, yes. Yes, Joey, it was."

A few days later, while Jim was clearing away the ice-covered debris of the fire, Aunt Maggie appeared with a blanket over her shoulders, and asked if she could speak to him for a moment or two.

"Why certainly." Jim jumped down from the

tractor. "But it's too cold for us to stand out here. Let's go into the barn."

In the semi-darkness of the barn, they sat side by side on a bale of straw.

"Jim," his aunt began, "first of all I want you to know how grateful I am to you for allowing me to stay here for such a long time."

He patted her hand. "We've enjoyed having you."

"Thank you for saying so. But last night I lay in bed thinking. And I finally said to myself, 'Maggie Newton, you're a selfish old fool.' "

Jim was about to protest, but she silenced him with a gesture and continued. "I not only invited myself to visit you, but I also committed the unpardonable sin of not leaving when I should have."

"But, Aunt Maggie, I told you before that you were welcome to stay as long as you liked."

She nodded. "I know, and that's where I've been selfish. I've just stayed on and on, because I've never been happier in all my life. If you can think of anything more improper than that, I'd like to know what it is. I came here in August, and here it is the first week in December."

"What of it?"

"Well, I'm ashamed of myself. I know in my heart that I should pack up and leave this very minute but" — a pleading note came into her voice — "Jim, dear, may I stay through Christmas?"

"Of course."

"I promise to leave the very next day," she added hastily.

Jim smiled. "It wasn't necessary to add that."

"Perhaps not. But I just wanted to assure you that

you won't have your daffy old Aunt Maggie on your hands for the rest of your life."

"There's nothing daffy about my 'old Aunt Maggie.' "

"Anyway," she continued seriously, "I was thinking last night how fine it would be to spend Christmas here with people I love. And, as I told you during the summer, I do love you and Joey, yes, and Pete, too — even if he is an old rapscallion."

Jim pursed his lips. "I'm afraid Pete hasn't disguised his feelings any too well about your presence here, and I'm sorry if he's made you feel uncomfortable."

"He hasn't really. Actually, he's been sort of a challenge to me. I find I'm continually trying to think up ways to win him over. But everything I do seems to rub him the wrong way. Perhaps he'll be happier when he hears that I'm leaving the day after Christmas."

"Maybe so. But anyway, Aunt Maggie, let's look forward to a real family Christmas. I'm sure it's going to be one of the best we've ever had at the Broken Wheel."

Aunt Maggie leaned over and kissed Jim's cheek. "Well, it's all settled, and once again I'm grateful to you. By the way, when will you be driving into town?"

"Tomorrow. Would you like to come along?"

"Yes. I'd like to do some Christmas shopping."

"I guess I'd better start thinking about that myself," said Jim soberly.

Pete was heard calling outside the barn. "Hey, Jim — Jim, where the heck are you?"

"In here. I'm coming right out."

Pete was armed with a shovel and a pickax. As Jim and his aunt emerged from the barn, Pete scowled at her and turned away. "I come to help you clear up this mess," he muttered. "If we don't git to it, it'll turn into a solid cake of ice."

Jim climbed into the seat of the tractor. "You're right, so let's pitch in."

"What was she gabbin' about?" Pete asked, after Aunt Maggie had gone into the house.

"Nothing that would interest you," said Jim with a straight face. "She wants to go back home, but I talked her out of it."

"Oh, is that all?" Pete lifted his pickax, then suddenly realized what Jim had said. "You *what?*"

"I talked her out of going home. I told her you'd be heartbroken."

Pete brandished the pickax. "How'd you like to git this thing right in the ear?"

Jim burst out laughing. "I wish I had a camera. The expression on your face would be worth a small fortune."

Pete wasn't sure whether Jim had been joking or not. "Was she really talkin' about goin' home? Tell me the truth quick!"

"Yep, she's even picked the date."

"When is it? Tell me!"

"The day after Christmas."

"Yer not kiddin'?"

"Cross my heart."

Pete yanked his hat off and skimmed it onto the roof of the barn. "Yip-pee!" he howled, dancing about gleefully. "That's the best news I've had in months!"

During the two weeks that followed, Pete was surprisingly civil to Aunt Maggie. He tipped his hat to her whenever they saw each other out of doors; he complimented her upon the crispness of the breakfast bacon; and one night, as she was retiring, he even went so far as to wish her pleasant dreams.

Although Aunt Maggie realized that the change in Pete had been brought about by the knowledge of her imminent departure, she could not help feeling pleased, and began thinking of some nice thing to do for him that would please him as well.

Four days before Christmas a magnificent idea finally occurred to her. Having learned that Joey and the men would be in town until dinnertime, she went into Pete's bedroom late in the afternoon and gave it a thorough cleaning. When the bed and bureau had been waxed and polished, she spread newspapers under Pete's favorite chair and proceeded to give it a coat of black paint. When the job was completed, she stood back to admire her handwork. Even the wicker seat was gleaming, and she turned out the light and went to the kitchen, filled with a sense of accomplishment.

When the men returned, she was busy preparing dinner and didn't hear them enter the house. As usual, Pete went straight to his room to take off his boots and put on carpet slippers. Although he noticed a peculiar odor in the room, he closed the door, went directly to his chair, and sat down. After tossing his boots into a corner, he rose to get his slippers from the closet, and discovered to his dismay that the chair came right up with him. As he reached down to disengage himself, his fingers closed upon the sticky seat. Pulling them away with difficulty, he looked at the palms of his hands and saw that they were black with fresh paint.

"What in tarnation!" he yelped. "Who the . . ."

His question ended in mid-sentence, as he realized that the chair was still sticking to the seat of his pants. Since his hands were already full of paint, he grasped the chair and yanked himself loose. Turning his back to the mirror on the door, he twisted his head around and saw the imprint of the wicker seat on the rear of his best trousers.

"Oh no!" he wheezed, not wanting to believe the mirror. "It jest cain't *be!*"

He brought his hands up to cover his eyes, then pulled them away quickly. In the glass he saw the black imprints of his hands on his cheeks, and his simmering anger came to a fast boil. Rushing to the door, he gave the knob such a rough yank that it came right off in his hand.

"Lemme outa here!" he roared, pounding on the door with his fists. "Jim! Joey! *Anybody!* Open this goldern door an' lemme outa here!"

Jim, Joey, and Aunt Maggie all arrived in the living room at the same time.

"Gracious!" said Aunt Maggie, startled. "I didn't hear you come home."

Pete's fists boomed against the door. "Where *is* everybody?" he yelled. "Jim! Joey! Where in tarnation are you?"

Joey ran to the bedroom door and opened it. Pete

almost bowled him over as he darted from his room, sputtering with rage.

"Hey," said Joey, laughing. "You've got black paint on your face."

"That ain't the on'y place I got black paint on, doggone it!" Pete turned around and bent over, pointing. "Lookit here! These is my good pants!"

Aunt Maggie gasped. "Oh, my goodness! I didn't get a chance to warn you."

Pete waved his finger under her nose. "I knowed it was you! I knowed you done this, the minnit I set down!"

"I'm so sorry, Pete. I'll do anything — *anything* to . . ."

"You done enough!" Pete yelled. "In four months you done enough to make this whole fam'ly miser'-ble! Why in blue blazes din you have sense enough to go home when yer welcome was wore out?"

"Hold it, Pete!" said Jim sternly.

Pete whirled. "Whattya mean hold it? You know in yer heart, Jim — an' so does Joey — the BW ain't been the same since this female come here bag an' baggage an' plunked herself down!"

"Stop that talk! Quit it! That's an order!"

Pete glared. "An *order?* Heh! Who do you think you are, a gen'ral or somethin'?"

"I'm boss of this ranch, and you're working for me. My aunt is a guest here and I won't have her insulted."

Aunt Maggie turned away, her eyes filled with tears. Joey took her by the hand and led her to a chair.

"Lookit her," Pete muttered. "She's jest like any

other female. When everythin' don't go her way, she busts out cryin'."

Jim caught hold of Pete's shoulder and spun him around. "I told you, you're not to speak that way to my aunt! This is my last warning!"

"Whattya mean yer last warnin'?" Pete stuck his chin out. "Whattya mean by that, Jim Newton?"

"You know very well what I mean."

"I shore do! You mean you'd fire me, ain't that what you mean?"

"I think you understand me."

Pete flung his arms out. "Okay, now we're talkin' plain! So before you say another word — *boss* — I'm goin' to save you the trouble! You ain't goin' to hafta fire me, 'cause I *quit!*"

With a contemptuous glance at Aunt Maggie, the angry old codger turned and marched back to his room.

"Aunt Maggie," Jim began, "I . . ."

"Please, Jim," she said, dabbing at her eyes with her handkerchief, "I've got to see about dinner. It will be ready very soon."

"All right," said Jim, "we'll talk this out afterward. Joey, you'd better go and wash up."

When dinner was announced, they took their places solemnly. As they ate their soup in silence, they were painfully conscious of Pete's vacant chair. While Jim was carving the roast, Joey asked to be excused for a moment and went to Pete's room. The old man had draped his trousers across the top of the bureau, and was attempting to remove the paint stains with turpentine.

"Aren't you coming to dinner?" Joey asked timidly.

Pete didn't look up. "Are you kiddin'?"

"We're having roast beef."

"So what? I wouldn't touch it if I was starvin' to death. That female's prob'ly poisoned it, anyways."

Joey returned to the table. "He won't come to dinner."

"That's his problem," said Jim. "Let him go hungry."

"Perhaps he'll eat later," Aunt Maggie said in a tiny voice. "I'll fix a plate for him and put it in the oven to keep warm."

None of them seemed hungry, and not even Joey asked for a second helping.

"There's chocolate pudding for dessert," Aunt Maggie announced. "Or Boston cream pie, if you'd prefer it."

"I'll skip dessert tonight, if you don't mind," said Jim. "I'm pretty full."

"So am I," said Joey.

Aunt Maggie folded her napkin. "As soon as I've cleared the table, I'd like to have a word with you both. And I'd like Pete to hear what I have to say."

Jim stood up. "All right, I'll ask him to join us, but I don't think he will."

"I'll help Aunt Maggie," said Joey.

Jim went to Pete's room and found him still dousing his trousers with turpentine.

"How's it coming?" Jim asked. "You getting the paint off?"

"Now there's a dang fool question if I ever heerd one. These here britches is plumb ruined." Pete rolled the trousers into a ball and fired them toward the wastebasket.

"We're going to have a family conference in a little while. I'd like you to be there."

"Wal, I ain't comin', so yap yer heads off by yerselves."

Jim shrugged. "Okay. By the way, if you want some dinner later on, it'll be in the oven."

"So what? It kin stay in the oven till it burns."

Pete went to his closet and took out a large duffle bag.

"What's the idea?" Jim asked.

Pete grunted. "Another dang fool question. I'm gittin' outa this nuthouse, that's the idea."

"Tonight?"

"Nope — first thing in the mornin', unless I'm heaved out."

"You know you're welcome to sleep here."

"Thank you very much," Pete said sarcastically. "I'll leave two bucks on the bureau fer the rent of the room."

Jim turned abruptly and walked out. In the living room he found Aunt Maggie talking on the telephone. Joey drew him aside.

"Jim, you'd better do something. She's calling the railroad for a train reservation."

Jim walked over to Aunt Maggie, who raised her hand for silence.

"Very well," she said into the phone. "That's for tomorrow, December 22nd, at 11:30 A.M., is that correct? Good. Thank you very much."

"Aunt Maggie," said Jim, as she hung up, "you

can't leave tomorrow. You were going to stay for Christmas."

"I'm sorry, Jim, but I won't be here for Christmas, as much as I'd been looking forward to it. My train leaves tomorrow at 11:30. Will you drive me to the station in the morning?"

"Of course, but can't I get you to change your mind? Please?"

"No, Jim dear. You're sweet to ask me, but my mind's made up. There's nothing you can do to change it."

Joey took her hand. "Please stay, Aunt Maggie."

"I'm sorry, Joey, but it's all settled."

Jim sighed. "Well, Joey, it's going to be a lonely Christmas, with just the two of us here."

Joey's jaw dropped. "You mean Pete's really quitting?"

"Yep, in the morning. He's packing his bag."

"Oh no, he can't leave. He's one of the family."

"You see?" said Aunt Maggie sorrowfully. "By thinking only of myself, I've broken up your family. I'll never forgive myself." A sudden thought occurred to her. "Jim, go tell Pete I'm leaving. Perhaps he'll reconsider."

"Not a chance. He's too bullheaded."

She twisted her handkerchief between her fingers. "It's all my fault, and I'm sick about it. I don't know what to say; I don't know what to do."

"Don't worry about it anymore," Jim said quietly. "What's done is done."

As Aunt Maggie rose from her chair, she suddenly seemed very small and helpless. "Well, there's nothing more for me to say. I think I'll go in and start packing."

"May I help you?" asked Jim.

"No, thank you." She took a few steps, then stopped, and turned. "Wait — there *is* something you can do. Will you come to my room please? You too, Joey."

In her bedroom Aunt Maggie opened the closet. It was piled high with packages wrapped in three different colors of paper and tied with red ribbon.

"Wow!" said Joey. "Are all these Christmas presents?"

"Yes, for you and Jim and Pete. I'd like you to take them out and put them around the fireplace."

Jim frowned. "Are you sure you want us to have them, after what's happened?"

"Of course. I chose them for you with a great deal of love. You can open them Christmas morning."

After the gifts had been arranged around the hearth, Jim said, "Wait here, Aunt Maggie. Joey and I have a few things for you."

They went to their rooms and returned with a number of gifts, which they placed on a table.

Aunt Maggie was misty-eyed. "Gracious, are all these for me?"

Joey nodded. "Mine are things you said you liked when we looked through the mail-order catalogue."

"Mine, too," said Jim. "Plus a few things from the department store in town."

His aunt sniffled. "I know they'll be just lovely."

"Would you like to open yours now?" Jim asked.

"I'd rather not, if you don't mind. I'll pack them in my bags, and save them till I get home."

"All right. I guess that would be best."

Joey knelt beside the packages on the hearth. "There're so many things here. How will we tell which is which?"

"By the color of the wrappings. The red ones are for you, the white ones for Jim . . ." she turned her head ". . . and the green ones are for Pete."

As they stared glumly at the gifts, they were startled by a sound at Pete's door. Turning their heads in unison, they saw Pete shuffle into the living room carrying three packages wrapped in brown paper. Without looking around, he bent over and placed them gently upon the hearth. With a shamefaced glance at the silent watchers, he straightened up and started back to his room.

"Pete," Jim said huskily, "come back."

"Later," the old man answered, in a tone scarcely above a whisper. "I still got some packin' to do."

"Are these your presents to us?" Joey asked.

Pete nodded, without turning. "There's one there fer each of you. The names is printed on the outside."

Aunt Maggie moved hurriedly across the room and took him by the hand. "Won't you stay with us?" she pleaded. "Just for a moment?"

Without protest Pete allowed her to draw him to the center of the room. She spoke softly to him.

"Won't you forgive me, Pete, for all the trouble I've caused?" He looked at her silently. "Please, Pete! I'm leaving in the morning."

"I know," he mumbled. "I was listenin'. I heard ev'ry word that was spoke."

"Well then, you know how I feel. Will you forgive me?"

Pete dropped his eyes. "To tell the truth, I'm the one that needs fergivin'. I oughta be hog-tied fer all them mean things I said."

"But you had a right to say them. They were all true."

"No they wasn't. Leastways they oughtn'ta been said in the first place. Yore a real, lawful member of Jim's fam'ly, but me, I'm on'y an outsider."

Joey spoke up indignantly. "You're *not* an outsider, Pete! Gee whiz, you were at the Broken Wheel even before *I* came."

"Joey's right," said Jim. "This is your home, Pete. You belong here."

Pete looked up eagerly. "You mean that, Jim? You really mean it?"

"You know I do."

"In that case," said Pete, with a sheepish grin, "I better go an' dump out my duffle bag."

"That's great!" Joey shouted gleefully. "I'll help you. Come on."

"Wait a second," said Pete, turning to Aunt Maggie. "How about you changin' yer mind, too, an' stayin' fer Christmas?"

Aunt Maggie smiled and shook her head. "Thank you, Pete, but I can't." She leaned forward and kissed his grizzled cheek. "Have a merry Christmas," she whispered.

His face turned a fiery red. "Same to you, Aunt Maggie."

Shortly before midnight, dressed in a heavy woolen bathrobe and fur-lined slippers, Jim went alone to the porch to have a look at the weather. The sky was a leaden gray, and a piercing wind was blowing down from the north. Shivering, he went back into the house and turned on the radio beside his bed. It was after two when he finally fell asleep, while listening to the grim warnings that were being broadcast throughout the mountain states.

Chapter 11
THE BLIZZARD

When Joey opened his eyes the room was filled with a white darkness. Thinking it was too early to get up, he rolled over and fell into a light, uneasy sleep. An unfamiliar sound brought him back to consciousness. It was the sizzle of bacon frying in the kitchen, two rooms away. Even when his door was open he had never been able to hear that sound before, but now it was closed. As he lay in a half-doze other small sounds reached his ears, all strangely magnified. A charred log in the living-room fireplace snapped in two; a drawer closed in Aunt Maggie's room; and a dry leaf, blown by the wind, scraped along the porch. Sitting up in bed, he looked at the clock and saw that it was five minutes past seven.

He stepped into his slippers, and went to the window and looked out. Beyond the porch, where the driveway should have been, was nothing but a whirling whiteness, and the porch railing wore a two-inch hump of snow.

He dressed quickly and went to the kitchen, where he found Pete cooking breakfast.

"Some surprise, huh?" said the old man.

"It sure is. When did it start?"

"A couple hours ago. No sign of its lettin' up, neither. It's a real son of a gun of a storm."

"Is Jim up?"

"Yep, he went out to feed the horses. Right after breakfast he wants to hitch the plow to the tractor an' clear the road as far as the gate."

"Where's Aunt Maggie?"

"In her room, gittin' dressed to go. She's already had her breakfast."

Joey rubbed a peephole in the steamed window-pane and looked out. "I can't see a thing. I wonder if Jim'll be able to get her to town."

"No tellin'. We'll hafta wait till we git a report on how bad the roads are."

Through the peephole Joey saw Jim's dim figure coming toward the kitchen door. Jim stomped the snow from his boots and came in.

"It's drifting pretty badly," he said with a shiver. "I'm afraid we're in for it." He took off his boots and mackinaw and placed them near the door. "How's Aunt Maggie doing?"

"She's gittin' ready," Pete said.

"I'd better get on the phone and check the road conditions."

Jim poured himself a cup of coffee and took it to his desk in the living room..

Pete motioned Joey to a chair. "You better git some grub under yer belt. How about some eggs an' bacon?"

"Swell."

While Joey was eating, Jim returned to the kitchen. "Bad news for Aunt Maggie. All the roads to town are impassable."

"What about the main highway?" asked Pete.

"There's been no traffic over it during the past hour. And the big plows won't be out this way until sometime this afternoon — if then."

"They'll never make it," said Pete.

"Her train leaves at 11:30 this morning," Joey said. "What'll she do?"

"Nothing. We're snowbound." Jim took a seat at the table. "How about some breakfast for me, Pete? The same as Joey's."

"Shore thing. Comin' right up."

They were discussing the storm as Aunt Maggie came into the kitchen, dressed for traveling. "I'm ready to leave whenever you are, Jim."

Jim shook his head. "Sorry, Aunt Maggie, but I've just checked the highway patrol, and the roads are closed."

She sank into a chair, dumbfounded. "Oh dear, what about my train?"

"You won't be able to make it. But they say the main highway might be cleared by this afternoon. I'll phone the station presently and try to get you a reservation on the night train."

"Please do, I'm all packed."

Later, when Jim attempted to make his call, he

164

found that the line was dead. "The wires must be down," he said. "We'll try again in a few minutes."

"Them wires won't be fixed fer a dog's age," Pete said. "Not in a blizzard like this."

Aunt Maggie paced the floor impatiently. "I can't understand why the weather bureau didn't warn us about the storm."

"It did," said Jim, "but not until after midnight. I listened to the radio reports until about two o'clock this morning. But the snow came so suddenly, no warning or prediction could have made much difference anyway."

He turned on the radio and they all gathered around it to listen. The news was grave. Cattlemen were warned to get their livestock under cover or into sheltered areas. The storm was expected to increase in intensity and last for several days.

Pete looked at Aunt Maggie from the corner of his eye. "Seems like you might be here fer Christmas after all."

"I'm sorry," said Aunt Maggie.

Joey grinned. "I'm not. I think it's great."

"Hold it," Jim said, as another radio report came in. "Let's listen to this."

The voices from the weather bureau droned on, bringing news of disaster. Railroad trains were stalled in three states, and most highways were entirely closed. The loss of life among livestock and wild game was expected to be in the tens of thousands. In one of the mountain states a farmer, who had been caught in the storm, had frozen to death while attempting to follow a fence to the home of a neighbor.

Jim turned down the volume and walked to the window. The snow had covered the second porch step.

"It isn't that bad here yet," he said. "Let's hope we won't get the worst of it, but we'd better be prepared anyway." He turned to Pete. "Get a reel of rope from the storeroom. We'll string it up from the porch to the barn."

"Smart idee," said Pete. "I'll meetcha at the back door."

"What are they going to do that for, Joey?" Aunt Maggie asked, as the men left the room.

"So we won't get lost the way that poor farmer did. After they string up the rope, we can follow it back and forth between the barn and the house."

"Oh dear, I never dreamed a snowstorm could be that serious."

When the men returned, Joey asked them whether they had gone inside the barn. "I'm worried about Fury and Angel," he explained.

"Fury's fine," Jim reported, "and Angel's lying down."

"She's goin' to have her foal real soon, if you ask me," said Pete. "Let's hope it won't come till this storm dies down."

As they listened to the radio, they learned that planes were in the air trying to locate stranded travelers. Those listeners who had two-way radios were requested to put them in operation, so that messages could be relayed in case of distress. Jim brought his radio equipment from the storeroom and set it up on the desk.

The first message that came through the speaker

was a request from a rancher who lived in an isolated section of the valley. He said that his youngest child was sick and needed a doctor's advice. When the youngster's symptoms were described, medical instructions were relayed to him at once.

After several messages of lesser importance had been delivered, the Broken Wheelers were shocked to hear a familiar voice.

"That's Mr. Lambert!" Joey said.

Chris Lambert was broadcasting an appeal for immediate help. His son, Packy, had been lost in the storm, and he was appealing to the people of the valley to assist him in finding the boy.

"Packy!" Joey cried. "Oh no!"

Jim snatched up his microphone. "This is Jim Newton at the Broken Wheel. Keep this band clear and let me talk to Lambert. If you hear me, Chris, come in."

"I hear you, Jim." The voice was husky and on the edge of panic.

"Give me the details."

"Packy's dog ran out of the house early this morning, before the snow was deep. Stella and I told Packy to stay home, but he disobeyed. While we were dressing, he saddled his horse and rode out." Chris's voice broke. "We haven't been able to locate him."

"How far have you looked?"

"A mile or so in each direction from the end of my road. The snow was too deep by that time to ride any farther, and I had a hard time getting home myself."

"Was Packy riding Lucky?"

"Yes."

"No tracks in the snow?"

"I saw what might've been tracks, going in your direction. But there were tracks the other way, too. I couldn't tell which way he finally went, because the tracks were filling up too quickly. Help us, Jim; we really need it."

"I'll do what I can, Chris. It'll take Pete and me a little while to attach the snowplow to the tractor. Meantime, keep in touch with Joey. He'll stay here by the radio."

"Right, Jim. Thanks for trying."

"Okay, Chris. Out."

"How long will it take them to attach the snow-plow?" Aunt Maggie asked, after Jim and Pete had gone.

Joey was only half-listening. "I don't know, pretty long. Poor Packy, it's awful bad out there. I can hardly believe it."

She squeezed his hand. "Don't worry, dear, they'll find him; I'm sure they will."

"But Packy's my best friend. I won't know what to do if . . ." Joey stopped and listened attentively.

"What is it?"

"A plane. Don't you hear it?"

She hesitated. "Yes, yes I do."

"It's not far away."

In a moment the plane roared over the house. Joey hurried to the window.

"I can't see it, but I can still hear it. I think it's circling."

Presently the plane buzzed the house again. As Joey listened, the sound of the engines faded away.

"I hope they're looking for Packy."

"Do you think they can see the ground?"

"I don't know, but they were flying about as low as they can."

Joey returned to the radio. As he was about to pick up the mike, a voice came from the speaker.

"Calling the Broken Wheel Ranch. Come in, BW."

Joey pressed the button. "This is the BW, Joey Newton."

"Now listen carefully, Joey. This is the CAA. That was one of our planes that just flew over you."

"Did they see Packy?"

"The pilot wasn't sure, but he saw some movement on the ground just south of your main gate."

Joey caught his breath. "How far south?"

"About a hundred yards. Are you equipped to make a search?"

"We will be soon. We're hooking up the snow-plow."

"There isn't time for that; it's snowing too heavily. If it is Packy out there, someone's got to get there in a hurry. Have you got a horse handy?"

"Sure, Fury."

"Okay, get going. Good luck."

Joey handed the mike to Aunt Maggie and started running. "Don't leave the radio!" he shouted. "I'll be back!"

It took him less than thirty seconds to put on his boots and mackinaw. As he rushed from the house, the wind struck him and almost blew him off his feet. Shielding his face with one hand, he found the rope with the other and followed it to the barn.

"Jim!" he cried into the swirling snow. "They

think they've seen Packy! I'm going to ride Fury down to the road!"

Hearing no answer, he realized that the men were in the tool shed working with the snowplow, but he had no time to get to them. The startled horses looked up as he raced into the barn. Opening Fury's stall, he called the stallion out and vaulted to his bare back. At the door, Fury saw the snow and whinnied. Once outside, Joey leaned down and slid the bolt. Bringing his knees together, he turned Fury into the deeply drifted road.

Fury's mane was white even before they reached the house and turned down the hill. The temperature was close to zero, and a fifty-mile-an-hour wind whipped stinging flakes into Joey's face. Fury lowered his head and picked his way gingerly through the drifts. It was impossible to see farther than a few feet in any direction, but as they came opposite the corral, Fury sensed that the fence lay to his left and moved close to it.

Joey buried his face in the snow-caked mane. "Follow the fence!" he cried. "Just follow the fence and we'll come to the gate!"

As the stallion floundered through the mounting snow, the gate finally loomed up just ahead. When they passed under it, Joey turned Fury left with the pressure of his knee. They were moving south now, with the wind at their backs.

Joey raised his head and called Packy's name at the top of his voice, but the sound was lost in the roar of the wind. He continued shouting as Fury pressed forward, stumbling and slipping.

Joey moaned. "It's hopeless; we'll never find Packy now."

After they had struggled for what seemed like an hour, Fury quivered and jerked his head up.

"What is it?" Joey cried.

Fury snorted and came to a standstill.

"Did you hear something?"

The long ears swiveled back, then shot forward. As Joey listened, he heard a faint sound that seemed to come from a point off to his right. Fury stiffened and gave a whistle. A second later the sound came once more — a strange sound that seemed like the whimpering of a dog.

Joey sat upright and called through his cupped hands. "Crosby? Crosby!"

Once again the whimper came, followed by Crosby's familiar howl.

Joey called eagerly. "Crosby! Where are you?"

Over the screeching wind the high-pitched howl turned into a series of hysterical barks.

"Packy!" Joey shouted. "Packy, do you hear me?"

Raising his forelegs high, Fury turned right and plunged through the deep drifts toward the sound of Crosby's continued barking. In a moment the barking was joined by the sound of a horse's terrified scream. Fury neighed in answer and, as they moved closer to the mingled sounds, Joey saw Lucky's dark outline in the gloom. Crosby was a gray ball floundering in the snow, but there was no sign of Packy.

Joey slid from Fury's back, landing waist-high in a drift. Calling Packy's name, he fought his way forward until he came to the wriggling, barking dog.

"Where's Packy?" he shouted.

Crosby yapped and scrambled to one side. Packy lay in the hole that the dog had vacated, and Joey realized that Crosby had been covering his master with his own body. Packy's eyes were closed. Joey brushed the snow from the boy's face and slapped him sharply on the cheek.

"Packy! Wake up!"

The small boy opened his eyes sleepily.

"It's me, Joey! Get up, Packy! Come on; you'll freeze!"

Packy smiled faintly and closed his eyes. Struggling for a foothold in the snowdrift, Joey grasped the boy by his jacket and pulled him to a sitting position. Packy made no effort to regain his feet, and Joey was forced to drag him to Fury's side. Finding extra strength that he never knew he had, he lifted Packy in his arms and boosted him to Fury's back, where the boy lay limp, faced downward. Slipping and floundering, Joey managed to draw himself up and throw his right leg across Fury's rump.

Fearful of being deserted, Crosby fought his way through the broken snow, howling like a demon. Joey leaned down and grasped him by the scuff of the neck and lifted him up, wriggling and whining.

"Lucky!" Joey yelled. "Lucky, come over here!"

The frightened horse whinnied and made his way across the trampled snow to Fury's side. Joey caught hold of the trailing reins and wrapped them around his wrist.

"All right, Fury!" he cried, gasping for breath. "Let's go!"

Fury stumbled, as he attempted to turn with the added weight upon his back. His body was steaming and the breath shot from his nostrils in two white plumes.

"Easy, boy, easy!"

Now they were facing directly into the wind and the stallion shook his head to get the blinding snow out of his eyes. The trail that he had broken on the outward journey was already partially obliterated, but could still be seen faintly. He followed it without further word from Joey, though it seemed as if they would never reach the gate. Although numb with cold and fearful of getting lost, Joey managed to keep his seat. Fury was pitching and tossing like a small boat in a heavy sea, and when he suddenly lurched forward into a deep hole Crosby slid from his back.

Joey let go of Lucky's reins and yanked the yelping dog up by his collar. Even without being led, Packy's terrified horse followed closely, walking in the holes that Fury's legs had dug.

When they approached the ranch gate, exhausted and half-frozen, Joey heard the chugging of a tractor. Fury brought his head up and gave a loud neigh. Jim and Pete were shouting, but their words could not be heard over the steady wailing of the wind. As Fury broke through the last white barrier and reached the level section of the road, which had been cleared by the plow, Joey closed his eyes and fell forward.

Jim caught him as he slid from Fury's back. Pete reached up and took Packy in his arms. With Joey lying across his knees, Jim put the tractor in gear and started up the road toward the house. Pete followed on foot carrying Packy, while Crosby, Fury, and Lucky followed them.

Aunt Maggie met them at the door and took charge immediately, with the calm efficiency of a doctor. She had prepared hot baths and medication, and ten minutes after their arrival, the two boys were in bed side by side with thermometers in their mouths.

When Pete returned from the barn, after having attended to Fury and Lucky, he found the sleepy boys telling Jim and Aunt Maggie about their adventure. Crosby lay at the foot of the bed, snoring like a small sawmill.

"How are they?" Pete asked anxiously.

"Aunt Maggie says they'll be okay," Jim answered. "No temperatures."

Pete sighed. "Thank the Lord. Did you tell Chris Lambert?"

Jim nodded. "The minute we found out they were going to be all right."

"What'd he say?"

"What do you think?"

Pete grinned. "I think mebbe he an' Stella went plumb nutty fer joy."

The boys were anxious to hear about Fury and Lucky.

"They're jest as healthy as you are," Pete told them. "No two horses ever got such special rubdowns."

Joey smiled and closed his eyes. "That's fine. Fury deserves everything that . . ." his voice trailed away

174

into nothingness. Packy had already drifted off to sleep.

Aunt Maggie motioned toward the door. "Let them sleep."

With a last look at the exhausted boys, Jim and Pete tiptoed from the room. Aunt Maggie pulled the quilt up gently, then bent over and kissed each boy on the forehead. Pulling a chair up beside the bed, she sat down and watched over them as they slept.

Chapter 12
CHRISTMAS

According to official reports, the blizzard was the most severe storm the mountain states had experienced in fifteen years. It raged for more than two days, and when the snow stopped falling on the morning of December 24th, thousands of families found themselves cut off completely from the outside world.

The United States Air Force moved quickly into the disaster area, and Operation Snowbound got under way. People who needed immediate help were directed by radio to signal their distress by spreading tarpaulins or colored blankets on the surface of the snow. When the signals were spotted from above, food and fuel were dropped by parachute. Acting upon information supplied by the airmen, bulldozers opened roads and dug out haystacks. Weasels — fast-moving vehicles equipped with caterpillar tracks — brought supplies of all kinds across the drifts to snowbound families. Thousands of men labored on the highways to rescue travelers who had been stranded in their automobiles.

It was learned later that some families had been forced to break up their furniture and use it as fuel, in order to keep themselves from freezing to death in their homes. Others told distressing stories of living on nothing but field corn for days. A few ranchers, whose homes had been entirely covered with snow, found that their only exit was through the roof.

When cattlemen broadcast the news that their livestock would starve unless fodder was brought quickly, airborne Operation Haylift began. Wherever cows were seen stranded in drifts, bales of hay were dropped to them from the sky. Although many animals starved before help came, numerous herds were saved by the Operation.

At the Broken Wheel, the north sides of the ranch house and outbuildings were buried in snow from ground to rooftop. Beginning at dawn on the 23rd, while the blizzard was still raging, Jim and Pete took turns on the tractor, clearing a narrow path from the house to the barn.

After the horses had been watered and fed, the men examined Fury and Lucky from head to tail to make sure that they had fully recovered from their grueling experience of the day before. They were gratified to find that they had suffered no ill effects. Angel, on the other hand, seemed exceptionally quiet and listless, and had very little appetite.

"I'm worried about this mare," Jim confided to Pete. "I wouldn't be surprised if she had her foal a little earlier than we figured. And if she has trouble, we might lose her."

Pete ran his hands along Angel's sides. "She don't look so good to me, Jim, an' that's a fact. When her foal comes, we got to help her all by ourselves. Doc Weathers is snowed in jest like we are."

"Well, let's hope there won't be any complications. And don't say anything to Joey about our being worried. If he asks how Angel is, we'll say she's doing nicely."

"Okay, Jim."

"One of us had better come out here every three or four hours to keep an eye on her. If her foal should start coming, we'll want to be ready."

"Wal, between the two of us we've seen many a foal born, so mebbe we kin pull Angel through, even if she does have a hard time."

When the men returned to the house, Packy and Joey were sitting up in bed being served breakfast by Aunt Maggie.

"Well," Jim said, "you two Arctic explorers look pretty chipper this morning. How're you feeling?"

"Great," said Joey.

Packy spoke with his mouth full of toast. "Me, too. We just woke up a little while ago."

Joey looked out the window. "What do they say on the radio about the blizzard?"

"It's still goin' great guns," said Pete. "Never kin tell when it'll let up."

"Did you get to the barn with the snowplow?"

"We sure did," said Jim, "and it was some job."

"Is Fury all right?"

"Yep, he seems fit as a fiddle."

Packy bit into a soft-boiled egg. "Fow's 'ucky?"

Jim frowned. "What'd you say?"

"Swallow that egg before you try to talk," said Aunt Maggie. "We can't understand you."

Packy chewed fast and swallowed. "I said how's Lucky."

"Oh," Jim answered, "Lucky's just fine too."

"And what about Angel?" Aunt Maggie asked. "The poor dear. I hope she's all right."

Jim and Pete exchanged glances. "She's doing very nicely," said Jim.

Aunt Maggie, who had a soft spot in her heart for animals of all kinds, was worried about the survival of the mustang herds out in the blizzard.

"They'll probably make out all right," Jim assured her. "During severe storms like this one, horses face into the wind and go to high ground. But cattle don't have much sense about such things. They let the wind blow them into fences or drifts, and many of them die without doing anything to help themselves."

Packy drained his glass of warm milk. "Hey, I wonder how my ma and dad are."

"As soon as you boys get up," said Jim, "I'm going to call them on the radio. How about it, Aunt Maggie? Do you think these two fellows are strong enough to get out of bed?"

"Yes, if they promise to rest and keep warm."

"I'm pretty warm right now," said Packy. "Boy, there's three heavy blankets on this bed, and a quilt besides."

When the boys were up and dressed, Jim spoke to Chris Lambert over the two-way radio.

"I know you and Stella are anxious to hear how Packy's feeling, so I'll tell you right off that he seems none the worse for wear."

179

"That's wonderful, Jim. Is he out of bed?"

"Yes, both he and Joey are sitting here by the fire."

"I don't want to tie up this wave band, but his mother would like to hear his voice. Will you put him on for a minute?"

"Sure thing." Jim handed the mike to Packy.

"Hi, ma," said Packy. "Boy, have you ever seen it snow so hard?"

"Oh, darling," said Stella, her voice sounding tearful, "are you feeling all right?"

"Sure, Ma; I feel great. But you know something, Crosby's sneezing. It's the funniest sound I ever heard."

"Your voice sounds strange, dear. Are you sure you haven't a cold?"

"No, honest. Jim's Aunt Maggie made us take about seven different kinds of medicine. If I did have any germs, they're all dead."

"I don't suppose we'll be seeing you for Christmas, sweetheart," his mother said dolefully. "We won't be able to get beyond the driveway for days. So will you try to be a good boy and do whatever Jim and Aunt Maggie tell you to do?"

"Oh sure. Save my presents till I get home, will you?"

"Of course, Packy dear. We won't celebrate Christmas until you come home, no matter how long it takes."

"I can hardly wait to tell you how Joey and Fury saved me," said Packy.

Jim took the mike. "Stella, this is Jim. We've got

to sign off now, so other people can use this barn. We'll get Packy back to you just as soon as possible."

Stella's voice broke. "We'll never be able to thank Joey enough for what he did. Good-bye, Jim."

"Good-bye."

For the rest of the day the boys stayed close to the radio, listening to distress messages and reports on the progress of the blizzard. Aunt Maggie watched over them like a visiting nurse, giving them hot soup and an occasional pill from her medicine kit.

Several times during the day, either Jim or Pete went to have a look at Angel, but her condition seemed unchanged. Joey was perplexed by the frequency of their visits to the barn.

"Why are you going out there so often, Jim? Is there something wrong with Fury?"

"Not a thing, Joey, I told you that this morning. We're just keeping the road open, that's all. You heard us using the tractor. If we don't plow every few hours, the snow will get ahead of us and we won't be able to reach the barn at all."

"That's right," said Pete. "An' I don't mind tellin' you, the seat on that danged tractor's beginnin' to feel like barbed wire."

Aunt Maggie packed the boys off to bed soon after dinner, and when they awoke in the morning the blizzard was over.

"Hey, you know something?" Packy said excitedly, as the family sat down at the breakfast table. "It's Christmas Eve!"

"Yes, it is," said Aunt Maggie quietly, "and by

hould be almost home in Philadelphia. But
I'm still here, I'm going to make this
look like Christmas."

"With all that snow outside," said Pete with a
chuckle, "it shore don't look like the Fourth of July."

"We always have a big tree at our house," Packy
said wistfully. "My dad always cuts one from the
woods in back of the house."

"Pete always does that for us, too," said Joey.
"But I bet you won't do that today, will you, Pete?"

"Nope, not unless I kin lasso one from the roof."

"Well, it wouldn't be Christmas without a tree,"
said Aunt Maggie. "It doesn't have to be a large one,
either; a small one will do. There's a little spruce
growing right beside the driveway near the kitchen
door. Jim, do you suppose we could bring it in?"

"I don't know why not. We could put it on the
table by the fireplace."

"That'd be great," said Joey. "I'll go out and get it
right after breakfast." He hesitated. "Wait a second.
What'll we trim it with? All the tree decorations are
out in the tool shed, and that's buried under about a
mile of snow."

"Don't worry about balls and tinsel," said Aunt
Maggie. "We're going to have the kind of tree I had
when I was a little girl."

During the morning, while the men and boys were
working outside with the plow and shovels, she bus-
ied herself decorating the living room. Old newspapers were cut into strips, then curled and pasted
together into long streamers, which were hung from
the rafters. Holly wreaths were cut from green card-
board and pasted to the windowpanes. Five of Aunt

Maggie's nylon stockings were dyed red and tacked to the mantelpiece.

During the afternoon, Aunt Maggie baked round cookies with holes in the middle and gingerbread Santa Clauses with beards of sugar. The Santas were stuffed into the stockings and the cookies were hung on the branches of the tree.

After dinner, while Packy and the men were put to work hanging more paper streamers, she took Joey aside and asked him whether he would mind sharing his gifts with Packy. Joey agreed readily, and before long, half of his packages, the ones wrapped in red, were sneaked from the pile, rewrapped in blue, and returned to the hearth without Packy's knowing it.

By ten o'clock in the evening the work was completed, and everyone sat down in the living room to admire the decorations.

"Wal, I'll be dadgummed," said Pete. "I ain't never seen a more Christmassy-lookin' room in my whole life. Aunt Maggie, you oughta git a medal from Ole Santa Claus himself."

Aunt Maggie blushed. "Thank you, Pete, but I couldn't have done a blessed thing without help. I want to thank everybody for having worked so hard."

"I wish my ma and dad could see it," said Packy. "Maybe they wouldn't feel so bad about me not being there tomorrow."

Aunt Maggie gave him a hug. "Don't worry, Packy. They'll have a second Christmas when you get home, and they'll enjoy it all the more because you'll be with them."

Jim looked at his watch. "Well, before Santa

comes down the chimney, I think I'll go out to the barn and see that everything's in order."

Pete shot a side glance at Joey. "I think I'll go with you, Jim. I wouldn't mind a breath of air before turnin' in."

"Let's all go," said Joey. "You, too, Aunt Maggie. We'll say merry Christmas Eve to Fury and Lucky and Angel."

Jim hesitated. "Well, okay, Joey, but we won't stay long."

Dressed in boots and sheepskin coats, they all trudged down the driveway between the towering banks of snow. The barn was silent and warm, and as they walked between the two rows of stalls, the horses watched them curiously, making small noises of welcome.

While Packy and the grown-ups stopped to talk to Lucky, Joey opened Fury's stall and went in. "Hi, there boy," he said. "Merry Christmas Eve."

The stallion jerked his head up nervously.

"What's the matter, did I wake you up?"

Fury snorted and craned his neck over the partition between the two stalls. Joey stood on his toes and looked over at Angel. She was lying on the floor, gasping for breath.

"Jim!" Joey cried. "Hurry!"

"What is it?"

"Angel! She's sick!"

Jim unlatched Angel's stall and knelt beside her. Her sides were heaving and her eyes were glazed with pain.

"Pete!" Jim shouted. "Come here quick!"

Pete came running. "What's wrong?"

184

"Angel's having her foal."

"Is she havin' trouble?"

"I'm afraid so."

Aunt Maggie pushed them aside and stooped down. "I'm afraid she's going to have a hard time," she said finally. "Jim, what kind of veterinary equipment do you have?"

"Pretty nearly everything we'll need." He looked up. "Joey, get the medical kit. It's on the shelf by the door."

Working with professional calmness, Aunt Maggie examined the heaving mare. "I'll need your help, Jim," she announced.

"What about mine?" said Pete.

Aunt Maggie looked up at him. "If you don't mind, Pete, I'd like you to take the boys to the other end of the barn and sit them down."

"What fer?" said Pete testily.

"Because I'm asking you to. Also, I want Angel to have as much quiet as possible."

The old man glared at her. "You shore you know what yer doin'?"

"Yes, Pete, I do. As I told you once before, I was brought up with horses. So if you want to argue with me, please do it later. Meanwhile, I'm going to do my best to save Angel and her foal."

The old man softened. "Wal, okay then." He reached down and patted Aunt Maggie on the shoulder. "Good luck. Me an' the boys'll be sweatin' it out over yonder."

For nearly two hours Pete and the boys paced the floor of the barn, while Aunt Maggie and Jim administered to Angel. Fury stood with his head over the partition, throwing his ears forward each time Angel uttered a sound.

It was a few minutes before midnight when Jim stepped out of the stall and beckoned. Pete and the boys came toward him quietly, suspense written on their faces.

"How is she?" Pete whispered.

Jim smiled wearily. "Fine — they're *both* fine."

"What is it?" Joey asked eagerly. "A filly or a colt?"

"A colt. Come and see."

Jim swung the door open, and they crowded about the entrance to the stall. Aunt Maggie was seated on the floor with Angel's head resting on her lap. Nestling against his mother's warm body was the slim, damp colt. His head and stockings were black, but the rest of his body was pure white.

Aunt Maggie stroked Angel's muzzle and looked up. "Well, Joey, what do you think of him?"

"He's wonderful! Just wonderful!"

"He's Fury's son. What are you going to call him?"

"I don't know, Aunt Maggie. I've got to think."

Packy grabbed Jim's wrist and looked at his watch. "Hey, you know something?" he cried happily. "It's just twelve o'clock!"

Joey smiled and fell to his knees beside the colt. "Hello, little Christmas," he said tenderly. "Welcome to the Broken Wheel."